DEATH IN THE DARK

A Sydney Rye Mystery, #2

EMILY KIMELMAN

For my parents, Don and Gay Kimelman, who are always there for me.

Lies, Truth, And Dares

"WAIT!" MY VOICE STRAINED AGAINST THE WIND BLOWING OFF the Sea of Cortez. I pushed through the sand, running after him. My dog, Blue, stayed by my side, his gait lopsided. Mulberry was a slow-moving figure several yards ahead of me. Solid looking in the hazy light of dusk, he took his time crossing the sand.

He didn't turn until I grabbed his arm. "Wait," I panted. "You're right. I need your help."

Mulberry grinned, pushing his crow's feet into sharp relief as his yellow-green eyes brightened. "I know," he laughed. "You're such a fucking mess."

Mulberry wrapped me in a hug with one strong arm around my waist and the other across my shoulders. He buried his head in my hair and pulled my face into his chest. At first, in that dark intimacy, I felt like I was suffocating. Almost immediately, though, I felt relief wash over me. I was not totally alone in this world; my only companion a limping mutt.

Blue yelped, excited by our embrace, and circled us, churning up the sand. Mulberry smelled like clean laundry, sea salt, and carried an unmistakable odor that was all him. Pulling away, he left his hands on my shoulders and looked down into my face. While Mulberry was only a little taller than me, it seemed like he was so much bigger, so much stronger and smarter, and under control. I felt like a blurry image next to his stark silhouette.

"Come on, I'll buy you dinner." He threw his arm around me and we walked back toward the Oyster Farm. I'd been living there for months, ever since we'd crossed into Mexico. I'd come for the oysters and had stayed for the isolation.

"So, where've you been?" I asked. "It's been what? Four months?" After turning our treasure into money, which made us both rich, Mulberry left, and I stayed at my Oyster Farm, despite his begging for me to come with him. "You went to Paris, right?" I asked.

The sun was beneath the sea now, and the deep blue of the sky was turning black at the edge. "Yeah, Paris, then London. Like I said, I've been setting up a business."

Back at my plastic table, a couple of oysters sat in their half-shells, waiting to be eaten. I righted the fallen bottle of tequila, but did not take a sip. The passport was there, too; dark blue and embossed with the American seal, it sat waiting for me to pick it up and become a new woman: Sydney Rye.

"Go on, take it," Mulberry said. "You might get carded at the bar." He laughed at his own joke, and I smiled.

"Yeah, right. That will be the day."

But I didn't pick up the passport. It suddenly felt like a betrayal to take on a new identity. I was, and should always be, the-fuck-up Joy Humbolt. Didn't I deserve the sentence I'd meted out to myself? Could a new name—a new life—change the darkness that lived inside me? It was the same darkness that haunted my every movement, and drove me to the brink of despair.

I laughed out loud.

"What?" Mulberry asked.

"I just don't know when I got so damn morose." I swiped at a tear that was suddenly moving down my cheek.

"You don't have to be, Joy." We waited in silence, listening to the gentle waves lapping at the hard-packed beach. A bird called out its final goodnight, stars popped out in the sky above us.

I reached out and toyed with the edge of the passport, peeking under its cover to look at the photo again. There she was, Sydney Rye: 5'6", blonde hair, scarred face, steel gray eyes. It would be my first passport. I'd never left the country before coming here. Well, fleeing here. Mulberry waited patiently for me to put the thing in my pocket, to accept that it was my only way out; I was no longer Joy Humbolt. She was a mess. Sydney Rye was a detective. I pushed it into the back pocket of my torn jeans, and turned to Mulberry.

"I'm ready."

At the bar, we were greeted by the owner, Andre. He was excited to see us again. "It's been too long," he called when we stepped under the awning. Andre, an Italian expat, hurried through the packed tables, his white linen shirt glowing under the soft lights strung above the patio. He shook Mulberry's hand with gusto. Andre's jet black hair, gelled into place, lay undisturbed by his large gestures. Spotting Blue, Andre reached over and scratched his ears vigorously. Blue accepted the petting gladly, and his eyelids drifted closed in pleasure.

Andre yelled at a waiter to clear a table near the front of the patio. "Margarita?" he asked me. "You must try my newest creation. And shall I bring you some food? Let me choose. I know what you love." Turning to Blue, he asked, "Have you had dinner yet?"

"He would love some dinner," I said. "And I'll take whatever you think is best." Mulberry nodded in agreement, and Andre hurried back across the patio into the small building where the kitchen pumped out steam, delicious smells, and trays full of food.

Blue settled himself under the table. A giant of a dog, his nose stuck out one end, while his tail stretched out the other. Blue had one blue eye and one brown, the markings of a wolf, the snout of a

Collie, and the height of a Great Dane. All these traits added up to a strange looking creature... at least that's how I see him. Other people—some might call them "sane" people—are afraid of him. Blue's overly protective nature and sharp teeth, which he shows off at even the hint of danger, don't tend to put people at ease.

Settled at our familiar table with Margaritas, chips, salsa, and several varieties of tacos on the way, Mulberry explained the plan. I was going to get some training down here in Mexico. "I know a great guy. He specializes in dogs. I met him at a conference about two months ago. I think you'll like him."

"Dog training?" I asked.

"Well, you guys are a team, right?" Mulberry looked at me over the top of his drink while he sipped off the dangerous top centimeters.

"Yeah, right, of course." I'd never thought of us as a "team" but Blue had saved my life. The bullet that shattered his shoulder was headed for me when he jumped in front of it. And I *did* pull him out of that pound in Brooklyn, so I guess we'd saved each other's lives once. Why not keep at it?

"After you've got a couple of months of physical training, I'm going to send you to work with an old friend of mine who is taking care of our interests in London. You'll love her. She's in her 50's now. Smart as a whip and totally brilliant."

"Sounds great." But really, I could not picture myself going through months of physical training, and then heading across the pond to work with some woman. It all sounded so unreal. But what was my life if not unreal? For most of the year, I'd lived in a haze of anger, sorrow, and regret. Maybe I could use a little fantasy.

"Remember the first time we came here?" Mulberry asked as our tacos landed.

"Sure. I think we had these shrimps then." I pointed to a plate of giant grilled tiger prawns Andre had sent over as a gift. I picked one up, expertly peeled it, and took a bite. I closed my eyes, and, for a moment, just appreciated the sweet shrimp, with its salty finish and perfect texture.

"It seems like a long time ago, doesn't it?" Mulberry said.

"Was it our first night in town?"

"No, it was our second, remember?" I thought for a moment, reaching back into my mind.

It was pouring rain, and my headlights barely cut the darkness when I rolled across the border between Arizona and Mexico. No one ventured out of the warmly lit hut serving as border control to check my I.D. They waved from the window at my RV to just keep driving. So I did. My relief was so intense that once the lights were no longer visible in my rearview mirror, I had to pull over. I climbed out into the storm, held my arms out to the side, and cried out into the void, "I made it!"

"What the fuck are you doing?" Mulberry pulled alongside me, leaning out of his open window, scowling. "Get back in the fucking RV. We're not there, yet." He rolled up his window and waited, looking straight ahead into the darkness. I climbed back into the sturdy old RV, and, soaked to the bone, started to drive again.

For three hours, we continued on the same road. Florescent-lit low buildings slid by in the darkness, advertising gas and tacos. My night vision made shadows into monsters, and the empty desert filled with motion. Part of it was the rain, so rare to that region that it seemed to delight in all the open space. Drops fell thick and straight, and then they came from the left, and suddenly from the right. My headlights, like a stagnant spotlight on a troupe of dancers, caught the movements in brief glimpses.

When we reached Puerto Penasco, the rain was gone, though it left the city a mess. The major roads were paved, but many of the side streets, especially those that ran along the ocean, had turned to mud. Mulberry, in the Jeep, sped ahead of me, fishtailing on the slippery surface. I could almost see the smile on his face. I followed at a more reasonable speed, though with little more control.

Mulberry turned into an RV camp, and I followed, nearly taking off a side mirror on the sign that read, "Playa de Oro RV Resort."

Inside the park, a stucco building meant to look like a welcoming hacienda housed the office. I saw Mulberry talking to a woman behind the counter. I waited in the truck. All around me, RVs rested in the dark. This was a place where people came for extended stays. Most of the RVs had tables and chairs set out with sun umbrellas. In one window, I saw a TV playing an old black and white movie. Most of the people here were retired, spending the winter of their golden years on the warm beaches of Mexico.

Mulberry stepped back out into the night and paused to light a cigarette. He'd started smoking again in, I think, Tennessee... or was it Arkansas? Either way, the tip of his cigarette glowed as he approached. "Got us a spot right on the water," he said. "I'll show you where." I nodded, and he moved off toward the Jeep. I couldn't see the water, but I could smell it, and if I strained, I could hear it over the rumble of my engine. Mulberry turned down a lane lined with RVs, and waved me toward an empty space, sparks flying off the tip of his cigarette.

I pulled into the spot and found myself staring out into the blackness that is the ocean at night. Turning the engine off, I listened to the soft lapping of the waves. A lump formed in my throat and tears burned in my eyes. It was all too much. I was filled with relief but also terror. Where the fuck was I and what the fuck had become of my life?

The sound of Mulberry hooking the RV up to the power and water supply snapped me out of it. I wiped my tears with my still damp T-shirt. Mulberry came in the side door and looking at me said, "You should change into something dry then we'll get something to eat."

Climbing out of the driver's seat, I passed through the living room and kitchen. Pushing aside the curtain that provided "privacy" for the bedroom, I smiled at Blue who was sitting up on the bed panting. Not exactly an amazing hiding spot for a giant dog, but we figured if Border Patrol boarded us, Blue was the least of our worries. I untied Blue's leash and he jumped down headed for the door. I peeled off my shirt, kicked off my sandals and struggled with my wet jeans, tipping onto the bed. I was sitting on more than just a mattress and some sheets. Underneath me was millions of dollars worth of stolen treasure. Gold coins, valuable jewels all hidden away in the most obvious of places: under the fucking bed.

I pushed my pants off. "Come on, I'm hungry," Mulberry yelled from the other room. Sitting up, I opened my closet and pulled out dry jeans and a dirty, though not wet, long sleeve. The only thing left in there was a rain coat. Funny, I thought, as I closed the closet door.

We took the Jeep back into the center of town and pulled over at the first restaurant we found. It turned out to be a tourist trap with nachos covered in iceberg lettuce and waitstaff that would rather be anywhere else on the planet. But we were delighted to be in Mexico. To be free of the cloying fear that chased us from New York across the country.

"It was some tourist trap right?" I asked Mulberry.

"Yeah, remember how horrible the food was. And Jesus, I've never had worse service." Mulberry picked up his Margarita.

I laughed. "It's amazing that the thing you remember most about that day is the terrible meal." I don't know if it was the Margarita, the stress, or that it was actually funny, but I laughed until I was no longer breathing.

———

MULBERRY LEFT the next afternoon promising that I wouldn't be alone for long. "I'm not alone," I smiled and rested my hand on the top of Blue's head, who leaned against my hip in response.

Mulberry nodded. "I guess I don't have to worry about you too much."

"Nah, I'm good."

"I know." He turned and looked at the sun, it was still high in the sky but dropping west. Sweat lined Mulberry's brow and dappled his T-shirt. His jeans looked heavy and hot in the bright day. Without a word he stepped closer to me and, wrapping an arm around my waist, pulled me into an embrace.

I put my arms around him and hugged back, resting against his solid form. It was hot and moist in his arms but it was also dark and safe. I pushed away before the tears welling in my eyes could escape. He kissed me on the cheek and I felt his stubble, just as much as could grow since the morning, it was the texture of fine sandpaper.

Mulberry got into his rental and headed through the dunes back to the main road. I stood in the sun with my hand shielding my eyes watching him go until there was nothing left to see but the yellow sand, blue sky, and circling sea birds.

I headed back to my RV. I'd kept it all these months, living in her for what seemed like a lifetime. The small shell was a safe haven for me. Inside was dark and cooler but still very warm. I plugged in a fan and laid down on my bed.

The fan clicked from one side to the other pushing around the still hot air. Blue panted in the other room and I felt like his breaths matched my heartbeats. I closed my eyes and let my mind wander until I drifted off to sleep.

In my dream I was standing in the front of the RV, in the kitchen area. The door burst open and a man with the head of a shark wearing an expensive grey suit stormed toward me. He had a gun and when he reached me I let him slap me so hard that I fell to the ground, landing on my stomach.

Turning over I looked up at him. His shark face morphed into a human face and then back to a shark. His gills pumped on his neck, red and glistening. The intruder had a gun pointed at my face. I turned and crawled away. He laughed behind me and kicked me sideways. That's when I saw a gun down the hall. I pulled myself toward it.

The shark man saw it too and tried to pull me back but I grabbed the weapon, relief swelling in my heart. I rolled onto my back and brought my arms up, the gun extended toward the hideous creature. He smiled at me, his mouth gigantic and filled with sharp teeth, his eyes human and filled with malicious joy.

I pulled the trigger, my heart pumping, my brain buzzing, relief crashing. But it just clicked against an empty chamber. The shark man's gills flared one last time before he shot me in the face and everything went black.

I woke with the sickening truth that sometimes your best isn't good enough. No matter how hard you try and how much you gain, sometimes the chamber is empty. I lay twisted in my sheets for a moment adjusting to the dark room. I could hear Blue snoring softly nearby. "Blue," I called. His head rose with a jingle from his collar and I heard large paws pad into the bedroom. Blue's silhouette filled the doorway, ears perked and head cocked. "Wanna go for a walk?" I asked sitting up.

He came around the bed and sat on the floor by my side. Blue leaned his long neck forward and rested his big head on my lap. Blue looked up at me and then sighing, closed his eyes. I rubbed his ear and ran my hand down his strong back. Blue wouldn't let a shark man shoot me in the face, I thought.

But it wasn't good enough. I got out of bed and walked into the kitchen. My gun, the one I'd bought in New York, sat in a drawer. I got it out and checked that it was loaded. Then I put it in my bag, making sure the safety was on. Finding a pair of flip flops I headed out the door. The horizon was still a dark blue and the night sky was just starting to show off its stuff. I walked toward town, through the dunes on a sandy road, itching for trouble.

There was a little secret I was keeping in my heart. A fact that I was afraid to think about but that haunted every moment of my day... even my sleep it seemed. When my brother was murdered I wanted revenge. And I went after it. I stole the man's treasure which had made me rich, a great thing if you want to waste your life away on a beach drinking.

The thing is I didn't just want that man's money. I wanted his life. It was mine. But I was too late. When I showed up he was already dead. Mulberry thought I killed him, the police said I killed him, the media was convinced I killed him, everyone thought I got my revenge but I didn't. Someone stole it from me. This left me with a sick urge, a need, an unyielding yearning to kill someone.

Blue and I made it through the dunes and stepped onto the paved road that ran into town. Cars drove by us, their headlights illuminating our way, showing off the dusty edges of the road. Large billboards loomed over us every quarter mile or so advertising new apartment complexes with names like *Sparkles* and *Golden Sands*.

A pack of stray dogs trotted out of the dunes. When they saw us they stopped and contemplated. Blue and I kept moving. There was nothing in them that would satisfy my needs. I didn't want to kill an animal, I wanted to kill an evil man.

When we reached the town I headed for the bar section. I knew it was dangerous walking around at night but I was hoping something would happen. I was begging for some schmuck to be dumb enough to fuck with me.

A couple of guys wearing plaid shorts and collared shirts, their hats on backwards, spotted me as they spilled out of a bar, blind drunk, and perpetually stupid. But before their verbal appeals for blow jobs could turn into something more sinister, their girlfriends, in minuscule skirts and teetering on high heels, tumbled out of the bar and pulled them away.

Past where the tourists drank I walked up into the crooked streets of the ghetto. Sand and broken bottles lined the road, sure signs that trouble lurked in the shadows. Maybe it was Blue or maybe I was so obviously dangerous that no one approached us, I spent hours wandering through the town but nothing touched me.

Eventually Blue and I went to a bar and I proceeded to get

hammered. Shots of tequila chased by cool, crisp beers soothed me and made sleep seem possible. We left the bar and headed for home. I was humming the last song they'd played on the stereo. I was off key but there was no one around to care. The night was warm, the stars bright, and I was headed home. The yearning was, for the moment, subdued. We left the lights of the town and started down the paved road toward the oyster farm.

I found my oyster farm soon after coming to Mexico while driving just to take a drive. Mulberry's guy had come for our gold and was to return with our money in a couple of days. Both of us were anxious and sick of each other and drinking. It was early and we'd had a spat, something about frying eggs in the RV being too stinky. I can't remember which side which of us was on but he'd gotten pissed and peeled out in the Jeep leaving me alone with the egg mess. Not to be outdone I decided to take a drive too. But I would be driving the Javelina.

As I bounced down the dirt road away from the RV camp, the stuffed javelina hanging from my rearview mirror swayed back and forth. The javelina is a pig-like creature that lives in the deserts of Arizona, New Mexico and Texas. As we crossed through their habitat parking in a different RV camp each night we heard tell of people spotting the small packs darting through the cacti at sunset. Their image was on mugs and T-shirts that read 'don't call me a pig.' Stuffed animals in their shape were sold at every truck stop we passed. It didn't take long for us to start calling the RV 'the Javelina' and it took only a day or two more for our journey to become the 'Javelina Trail.'

Maybe that is why we were fighting, I thought, as I moved through the crowded streets of Puerto passing women in tight clothing and men fanning themselves in the shade. Maybe because the Javelina Trail was coming to an end.

After leaving the city I drove parallel to the ocean in what looked like a desert. That's the thing about Puerto Penasco, it's ocean front but you'd never know it unless you were looking right at the sea. The sand stretches back to the U.S border and beyond. I could see how a person wandering in those never-ending dunes could stumble onto the shores of the Sea of Cortez and think it was a mirage. The sparkling turquoise water does not belong in the middle of a land so parched.

The sign for my oyster farm was hand painted and featured a topless mermaid pointing with a mollusk down a sand road into the dunes. The next sign was for condos named *Sparkles*. There was something about the oyster farm's sign that was utterly appealing when compared to *Sparkles'* grand dream of a tall building with Jacuzzi tubs and granite countertops. All the ostiones farm was offering was oysters and topless mermaids. And if you don't like those two things then we are probably not going to get along.

I turned down the road and hit the gas to keep the Javelina from sinking. Soon the paved road was gone from my mirrors. All I saw was the beige sand rising and falling where the wind last left it. I didn't see the small piece of wood with the word 'Ostiones' and an arrow painted on it until I was almost past it. It was a tight turn and I had to back up a dune to make it. I hit her into reverse and sped up the side of the sand mound and then knocked it quickly into drive. I could feel the back wheels sinking and I saw sand spitting up behind me as we rolled down the dune and onto the path leading to oysters.

There was nothing in all directions as I bumped along; just me, my old RV, sand and the big blue sky. I hit a bump and heard the unmistakable sound of egg shells cracking. Looking back into the kitchen/living room I saw the remaining half dozen eggs broken on the floor. Blue wobbled back and forth with the jerky movements of the RV while trying to lick up the spilled yolks. When I turned forward the Sea of Cortez was sparkling before me.

I braked hard, coming to a stop next to a very basic structure fronted by seven plastic tables and chairs that were open to the air but shaded by a palm frond roof. A breeze blowing off the sea played with the straw and made the place look deserted. The sound of Blue licking at the eggs and the gentle hum of the engine filled the Javelina.

A man stepped out of the simple concrete structure squinting against the sun. He was of medium build, but clearly strong. His skin was brown and looked like it had spent more than its fair share of time in the sun. He looked over at the RV sitting in his driveway. I waved and he waved back. Climbing out of the Javelina, I smiled and called, "Hola."

He walked toward me gesturing to one of the tables. Blue followed behind me. The man did not flinch. He just nodded to Blue as though another human was with me.

I took my seat and Blue crawled under the table. "Ostiones?" I asked. The man nodded and moved back to the shack. The beach curved around forming a small inlet filled with bright blue water. Directly across from me the beach rose up into a sand dune. The wind played with its tip sending sand cascading down the dune's side.

The man returned with a dozen oysters on a tray and a Corona. I smiled at him and pointing to myself said, "Joy."

"Ramon," he answered. Ramon left me and I ate my oysters and drank my beer while staring into the Sea of Cortez.

I hadn't left and Ramon never questioned that. It was as if he was expecting Blue and me. He lived with his mother in the cement house and we lived in our RV. I started paying rent after a week, though no one ever asked. I just started leaving a couple of hundred bucks as a tip. I liked it there.

But I knew it would not last. You can't spend your life on the beach eating oysters and feeling bad. Sometimes you have to make a change. And that night, when I flopped drunk and exhausted onto my pathetic mattress, I knew something was going to give.

2

Wake Up!

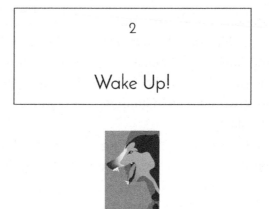

I WOKE UP WITH MY HANDS OVER MY HEAD, THE JOINTS AT MY shoulder aching. It was hot in the small space and I tried to scratch an itch on my nose but couldn't move my arm. I blinked my eyes open.

There was a man sitting on the end of my bed. Instantly I was awake and nauseous with fear. I yanked at my arms but instead of moving them down to me, I moved myself up to them. Sitting on the bed, my feet underneath me I could see that my hands were tied and stuck to the headboard with what looked like a giant nail. My ankles were bound with a thick rope that itched once I saw its rough fibers rubbing my skin red.

The man was small in stature, thin, with black hair that curled in tight ringlets almost to his waist. His skin was tan and his eyes deep brown. His eye lashes curled up, long and thick, like a cow's. He watched me without comment.

"Who are you?" I asked, my voice rough.

He smiled, a wide grin that showed off big teeth with even, thick spaces between them. "I'm Merl."

"What are you doing in my bed?"

He reached out a hand and that's when I saw the dogs. There were three Doberman pinchers patiently panting. Two on his left and one on his right. Blue sat next to the last, his pant in sync with theirs. Merl reached into his belt and pulled out a knife.

I breathed deeply, trying to slow my heart which was in the process of filling me with so much adrenaline that my teeth began to chatter uncontrollably. I clenched my jaw to shut them up and felt my stomach threatening to empty.

"Cat got your tongue?" Merl asked and then laughed, showing off his wide-set teeth again. The knife glinted in his hand. Merl reached toward me with the knife. When his head was close enough, I reared back mine and tried to slam it into his skull. But Merl was much too quick for me and I threw myself through the air, flipping off the bed.

Getting my bound feet underneath me I faced him, my teeth grinding and my heart about to explode.

"You're even better than Mulberry said," Merl told me from the end of the bed. How did he get all the way down there?

"What?" I asked.

"Mulberry sent me," he said.

"Mulberry sent you to tie me to my bed and threaten me with a knife?"

He shook his head.

"You're the trainer?" I asked, the fact dawning on me.

Merl nodded. "And I brought help." He pointed to the three dogs. "Thunder, the oldest and most faithful of my companions." The first dog stood and barked. His slick black coat shone in the dull light that filtered through the RV's small windows. There was a sprinkle of grey on his formidable muzzle. "Michael, the largest of my friends." The middle dog stood and barked a welcome, his tongue lolling out of his head. He was a giant, not as tall or thick as Blue, but it looked like he was carved from pure black granite. "And Lucy, the smartest dog that ever crossed my path." Lucy stood and wagged a small nubbins, the remainder of her cropped tail. She was not as big as Michael or as wise as Thunder but there was something in the dog's eyes that made me think she might be the most dangerous of the three.

"I see you've met Blue," I said, still standing in my underwear and torn T-shirt with my wrists and ankles bound.

"If I let you free do you promise not to try to headbutt me?" Merl said, his eyes all smiles.

"Ok, but I think you should realize that was a pretty normal reaction." Merl laughed as he came around the bed. He leaned across my pillows and cut the rope on my wrists. There were soft red lines but nothing permanent. "I think there were a couple of factors that made me think you were here to hurt me. Like the binding and the knife."

Merl leaned over the bed and cut the rope around my ankles. I stepped away quickly and pulled a pair of pants out of my closet. I slipped into the oversized jeans and pulled the belt tight.

"You know you kind of dress like a hobo?" Merl said and cocked his head. I looked over at the four dogs and their heads were all cocked too.

"That's a compliment coming from a guy dressed like one of the Columbine shooters."

Merl laughed heartily at that. He was wearing a black T-shirt tucked into black jeans and I just bet there was a matching trench coat somewhere in his car or tossed over the couch in my living room.

Now that I was no longer in mortal danger I could feel that I was hungover. My head was banging and the nausea I'd experienced was not subsiding. "I need a glass of water," I said pushing past all the fucking dogs into my living room. The place was a mess. I hadn't done any dishes since Mulberry's arrival and he hadn't done any either. Another reason the two of us living in an RV together hadn't worked out.

I pulled out a bottle of water from the fridge and took a long slug. The small space smelled like dogs panting. I pushed open the door and stepped out into a cloud-covered day. A cool breeze was blowing off the sea and I walked toward it. Blue leapt out after me and ran toward the beach. He jumped into the small surf and turned to me, his ears and tail high with anticipation.

The other three dogs followed Merl out. They flanked him like tigers in a circus show. "Free," Merl said, and the dogs took off, black streaks of speed against the beige sand. They barreled toward Blue and soon it was a just a mess of dogs in the surf, rearing up against each other, teeth to neck fun time.

"You like to play like your dogs," I said, then took another sip of the cold water.

"What do you mean?"

"Playing at killing each other."

Merl laughed. "Very well put, Sydney. Very well."

He was the first person to call me Sydney without ever calling me Joy.

"Let's get some food," Merl suggested. "Do they serve breakfast here?"

I nodded and we walked over and sat down at one of the plastic tables. Ramon came out and waved to me. "Huevos, por favor," I called. He held up two fingers, I nodded. Ramon went back in the house.

"Interesting set up you have here," Merl said.

"It's been working."

"But not anymore?"

I took another sip of my water. "Maybe."

Ramon's mother, Abedella, came out with a pot of coffee and a big smile. She placed mugs in front of each of us and poured the first steaming cup. We thanked her and she headed back into the house.

"You do that often? Tie women to their beds?" I slurped my coffee hoping it would revive me.

"I wanted to see what you were like. We reveal a lot about ourselves when surprised."

I put down my coffee cup. "Not the best way to build trust, is it?"

Merl leaned back in his chair. "Maybe." A smile played on his lips.

"Is this the kind of behavior I should expect from you?" I asked.

Merl laughed. "You shouldn't ever expect anything. Let that be the first thing I teach you."

"Teach me," I grumbled.

"Yes, Sydney, teach you." His voice softened. "I'm not just here to train you on how to throw a punch or have an effective partnership with Blue. I'm here to show you how to think." He tapped his temple. "It all starts up here."

"Well, up here," I touched my own head, "I'm pretty pissed you tied me to my bed!" I didn't mean to shout but that's how it came out.

Blue paused in his play and came to my side. Merl leaned back in his chair and put his hands behind his head. "Impressive," he said. "You can yell." His words dripped with sarcasm and I wanted to fly across the table and yank his ridiculous long hair. His eyebrows jumped. "Any other skills?"

"Fuck you," I stood up, Blue's hackles raised.

Merl didn't say anything until I'd turned toward the RV. "Why do you think you're here?" I looked over my shoulder at him. He gestured around to the Oyster Farm: the Port-a-Potties on their raised platforms, the aged RV sunk into the sand from lack of use, the two-room shack Ramon and his mother shared.

"What do you mean?"

"What happened? In your mind, why are you here?"

"I made a big mistake," I said. He nodded. "If I'd just done my job and ignored the dead body in the alley, I would still be living in my rent-controlled apartment hanging out with my brother." My voice broke on brother. I looked past Merl and out to the sea with its gentle persistent waves and reflective surface. I watched the sunlight crest with each swell. Blue leaned into me, pushing his muzzle against one of my hands.

"One of the biggest mistakes we can make is spending too much time thinking about our mistakes. Just acknowledge what you did wrong and move on," Merl said.

"I should just mind my own business" I said.

"Is that where you made the mistake?"

"Yes."

"Really? I thought it was your ego. I think you underestimated who you were up against."

"I didn't know who I was up against."

"Another mistake, not figuring it out quicker. You should have killed him in the basement when he laid on the ground at your mercy."

I was still looking out at the sea and his logic struck me with the power of a blow. Of course, that's where my mistake was. It wasn't that I let him get away in my apartment, or that I went looking for him in the first place. I had the chance to end him as soon as I knew he was a monster and I didn't.

I turned to Merl. "You see?" he asked. "You can ask as many questions as you like, as long as you're ready to make decisions once you get your answers."

"Merl, who are you?"

He laughed. "That's an awfully broad question. Please sit down."

I hesitated for a moment but the steam coming off my cup of coffee convinced me to start again. "Okay, I'll ask a better question," I said as I slid back into my chair. "Were you in the army?" Merl nodded but didn't elaborate. I looked at him for a moment and then asked, "What was your poison?"

He smiled and with a teasing twinkle in his eye said, "What do you mean?"

"Your hair's too long for someone without an addictive past."

He laughed softly. "Not sure about that, but yeah, heroin. It held me pretty tight at one time. Couldn't get free of it until the dogs."

We both turned to look at where his dogs played in the surf. Blue followed our glance and sprinted off to join the fun. "The dogs. Did you learn that in the army?"

"No, I was a basic training kind of guy. Pretty strong for my size, fast in a fight." He smiled and mimed a quick one-two punch. "But no, I was unemployed after the army kicked me out for my addiction. But you know, they didn't call it that or they would have had to give me some treatment. They called it exhaustion and gave me a ticket home."

"Really?"

He shrugged. "Sometimes that's what happens."

"But so how did you get involved with dogs?"

"After I left the army I was all strung out. I'd been posted in Japan and a friend of mine, an ex-addict himself, pushed me to get treatment. He sent me to China to this place in the middle of nowhere. There were these crazy mountains," he sat up tall and spread his hands like he was showing me the size of a big fish. "They were the kind that look like one half of a giant narrow oval. You know what I'm talking about?"

"I think so."

"And they were all covered in vegetation. 'How is that possible?' I thought when I first got there. How can something grow there?" He shook his head. "To get there we drove on this rutted dirt road for hours. I thought I would die. I mean I was going cold turkey. You should not be bumping along a dirt road in an old van that lost its shocks years ago when you are going cold turkey." He laughed. "It will fucking kill you. By the time I got there I must have been half dead. I thought I'd died and that it was heaven." He laughed again. "It's funny that I thought I would go to heaven, a junky with no loyalty."

Merl shook his head and played with the edge of his coffee cup. "It was this big white building that just kind of rose out of the river bank. The road was a slick, muddy mess but somehow this white building was totally clean. There was a large wooden deck that stuck out over the water and there were all these people in silk pajamas practicing Tai Chi. Of course, at the time I didn't know that's what it was called. I thought it was some kind of dance. I was so fucked up that when I got out of the van I immediately threw up." Merl shook his head. "I was a mess," a sheepish smile crossed his face before he continued. "The most beautiful woman helped me up to my room. It was narrow with a small window that looked out over the river and a single bed that felt like it was made of nails. I was delirious. Absolutely delirious. I thought that maybe the mountains were filled with heroine and that if I climbed out the window I could go to them. But," he bit his lip and shrugged his shoulders, "she was always there to stop me. This woman had incredible strength. I remember thinking that she was much stronger than me and that it must be the dancing. Or the fighting. Whatever that thing was that they were doing. I thought that was why she could move me around."

He laughed again. "And maybe it was that but it also could have been that I was little more than a bag of bones. The bathroom and my room were the only places I went for the first week. Once the fever broke, that woman, whose name was Mei-Ping, took me outside. I remember not wanting to go but she just smiled at me. It smelled so sweet, the air out there. My room was putrid and stifling, I realized, once I stepped out to the river bank. Mei-Ping mimed that I should wash myself in the river, which, by the way, was like this big muddy spill. I mean it was hardly better than the road. But I did it. At this point Mei Ping was my guiding light. She had control over me and not just because she was so strong." He laughed deeply at that one. "No, she was so soft, you know? She really taught me about the different aspects of strength. It's not about how much you can lift but about how calm you can be.

"I washed in the river. Which made me pretty dirty really, but I think she was trying to baptize me in a sense. I needed to wash away the old me and it had to be done in a way that would leave me dirty. You can't ever be clean. There is no salvation really. I don't know what happens after we die. Maybe when you go to real heaven the water is clean and takes away all your sins. But this river water just washed me dirty. It helped me let go of what had happened. The slave I'd been, the trusts I'd broken."

Merl paused and looked toward the cement house. "I like a beer every now and then but that's it for me. Nothing else. I can't trust myself. And I don't know how many chances you get. How many rivers can cleanse you with mud. I'm not sure of the numbers but I doubt I'd get another chance. And I'm not one for throwing away chances. Not anymore anyway."

"So that does not explain how you started training dogs," I said.

Merl turned back toward me and continued. "After I washed in the river Mei-Ping washed me in a real bath. Got me all clean. And this was water she'd boiled in a pot and then poured over my head. She was an angel, I'll swear to that if nothing else in my life. I've met an angel."

"Ok, so you were in love with her."

"No, no." He shook his head and waved his hands at me. "She was so far above me. You can't be in love with someone so much higher than you." Merl's eyes were wide and he looked up at the palm fronds above our head. "She was too much for me. Sure, I loved her but to be in-love you have to, or at least I have to think of that person as amazing, wonderful, all those things, but on my level." He looked back down at me. "You're not in-love with God. You worship him, you love him, but there is no boning about it. And being in-love definitely includes boning. Right?" He cocked his head at me.

I laughed and reached for my coffee. "Sure, OK, so you were not *in-love* with her. You loved her but no boning."

He laughed. "Yeah, no boning. Anyway, I spent months there getting stronger. Mei-Ping started to teach me Tai Chi which is really what gave me the strength I needed. I'll teach it to you. In fact, we'll start that today."

"Very Mister Miyagi of you."

Merl ignored me. "I stayed there for almost 8 months. I had some contact with the outside world but not much. It's not like there was a computer there. I'd let my parents know where I was and my mom sent me letters telling me about what they were up to.

"They had moved to a small town in North Carolina from the house I grew up in Delaware. My Dad joined a country club where he could golf and my mom had her gardens and they were really happy.

"But then she wrote that she was worried about Dad. He was going to have surgery and wouldn't I please come home." Merl paused and looked over at Blue and Thunder wrestling in the sand. "You know what? There was a moment where I was terrified for myself when I read that." He looked back at me. "I didn't know if I could stay me once I left that little paradise. There were no temptations there. I was without conflict. I did my duties, I practiced my practice. I did not have any old wound openers. And mind you, I had a pretty good relationship with my parents. We weren't big sharers or anything but we all loved each other and knew it. I was just afraid that the old me would come back. But, those thoughts only lasted an instant. I knew that what I was really facing was my father's death and I needed to go home immediately. It took only a couple of days to get there."

The door to the house opened and Ramon stepped through holding two plates of food. He shuffled his feet through the thick sand and placed the plates, brimming with refried beans, tortillas, cheese, red sauce, and all topped with a fried egg, before us. His mission accomplished, Ramon broke out into a wide grin.

"Looks amazing," I said and gave him a thumbs up. Merl nodded and smiled too. Ramon returned to the house. I refilled my coffee cup and Merl's.

"We need-" Merl started.

"He'll bring them," I said.

Merl turned to look at the house. There did not appear to be any movement inside. I sat back and sipped my coffee watching Blue pant in the sun. Two of the Dobermans wrestled nearby. Merl sat back in his chair, coffee cup in hand, and joined me in watching the dog show.

I heard the door open and turned to see Ramon hurrying across the sand with napkins wrapped around cutlery. He started to apologize but I wouldn't let him say a thing. "Gracias, muchas gracias," I said, taking mine from his hand. Merl took the other and we both dug into our breakfast. My plate half empty I sat back and took a breath. I wiped my mouth and crumpled the napkin.

"So you left to go see your father, then what happens?"

Merl smiled and swallowed his bite, wiped his mouth and continued his story. "I'd arrived with a small bag and I left with an even smaller one. Mei-Ping took me to the airport and she kissed me goodbye the way a master kisses her grown puppy, with pride and joy at what I'd become." He sipped at his coffee and cleared his throat. "Being on a plane and re-entering the normal world was so strange to me. Last time I'd faced security, I was sweating and dying and fighting myself at every turn. Now I was this fluid creature. Nothing got in my way because I was following the energies of the room. In Tai Chi we learn to use the energy of our opponent against them. This is what I was doing with everything. It was like I was floating and all the people around me were crawling.

"When I landed in New York and was transferring to head down south, I ran into an old army buddy. He was gregarious and excited to see me. He lifted me off the ground with his hello hug. I saw what I had been in him and I was happy to now be me. There was this deep anger in him and that was what made his motions so big, his smile so large. We went to a bar and he downed beers like they were glasses of water and we were just back from a trek through the desert.

"Within a half hour he was drunk. I convinced him to take his leave in China at my retreat instead of going home. I paid for his ticket and told him to find Mei-Ping. I think the world would be a much better place if we all got to go spend some time with Mei-Ping."

"Sign me up," I said with a smile.

He laughed and shook his head. "I headed south and my mom picked me up at the airport. She was drawn and scared but putting on this big show of bravery for me. It broke my heart to see her trying to protect me. I took her in my arms right there in the airport parking lot where she was chattering on about how my father was going to be fine and this was considered routine in men his age and I should really not worry but she was glad I was there.

"I'm not a tall man but my mom is smaller. She kept talking at first. But I pulled her close. There was not really anyone around but it was still the most affection we'd ever shown in public. In fact, I think it was the longest hug of my adult life. She stopped talking. Well, really the talking just turned into these hiccup tears and I could feel that she was terrified. So scared that she would lose the one man she'd had all these years. The one thing that she was living for, cooking dinner for, having kids for, and now he was laying in a hospital room strung up with wires and tubes and beeping machines and no amount of freshly-made beds or spotless kitchen counters could save his heart.

"I didn't tell her to shush, I didn't rub her hair I just stood there like one of those oval mountains and let her cry onto my chest. We didn't talk about it after. That's not the kind of family we were." He laughed again. "Not that we were the type of family to stand around in airport parking lots crying but if we were going to do such things we were not going to talk about it after. And I was fine with that. I don't think we have to talk about every emotion that crosses our souls.

"We went straight to the hospital and there he was: my dad, the biggest, strongest guy around. But now he was so much smaller. Almost my size. He smiled and I recognized his spirit. But it was clear the guy was not going to make it. There was no beating time. You can't fix it, tape it up, extend it. Time does not allow itself to be challenged. It keeps going and you don't. And that is life."

"That's a sunny outlook," I said.

Merl shrugged. "It's not an outlook, Sydney, it's just a fact."

I pulled at a piece of tortilla and rubbing it around on my plate said, "I guess."

"I practiced in the hallway of the hospital outside of his room. I practiced in my parent's backyard so filled with my mother's wonderful gardens. I practiced everyday. I didn't let my teaching go and that is why I was able to stand it. It is a part of our lives to lose our parents and through my practice I was able to find peace with that."

I thought about the passing of my own father briefly and then shoved the memories away. There was no peace there for me.

"Of course I mourned my father," Merl continued. "At his funeral, which was well attended not only by his old friends, but also the new ones he had made in his southern community, I cried as he was lowered into the ground. I let my loss express itself. You can't hide from time and you cannot hide from grief. So I let mine out, holding hands with my mom who cried, too.

"At the reception a man about ten years younger than my Dad approached me. He said he knew my father, they were golf buddies, that my father was a really good man. I agreed. 'You need a job?' he asked. I was taken aback but answered that honestly I did. My mother and I'd spent all our time at the hospital and running around. I had not thought about my next move, but yes, I realized I should stay here with my mom, get a job and help her find her new place alone in this world.

"He owned a dog training facility. And not just any dog training facility. He trained dogs for the army, for police departments, and of course, for rich families who wanted a well-behaved pooch. He taught me his trade. Really though, Mei-Ping taught me his trade. I was calm, I didn't push back, just let them use their own energy to do my bidding. I excelled there. For 15 years I trained with that man, Abraham Wilkens. We became very close.

"However, when my mother passed away," Merl picked up his napkin and toyed with it as he talked. "She died in her garden, a small cough, a gentle collapse into blossoming poppies, and she was gone. My dog, Thunder, who'd been keeping her company sat by her side, licked her face, and cried until I got home. It comforted me to know she was not alone in the garden where some creature might have found her."

Upon hearing his name Thunder separated from the other dogs and came to Merl's side. Merl reached out his hand and brushed some sand off the old dog's muzzle.

"I didn't want to stay once she was gone. The house was just so empty and it was time for me to move on. Abraham understood. I've been working freelance like this ever since."

"Like this?

"Yup," he smiled and shook his head. "No, few of my cases have been like you. No one has ever had the raw talent."

"Raw is right."

"Raw is best."

3

Training Montage Time People

RUNNING ON THE BEACH WITH BLUE BY MY SIDE BECAME MY every morning. Merl ran behind us, his dogs flanking him. We'd run so far and so long that by the end I wanted to dive into the water, sink under the gentle waves, and be washed clean the way Merl was in China. But it felt like the fever inside of me would never break. I'd never be on the other side of this thing.

We practiced Tai Chi at dusk, once the sun was calm enough. "Relax," Merl would say, and wiggle my extended fingers. "Don't rush," he'd remind me as I tried to float across the sand. "Relax," he'd say, and touch my shoulders to make me drop them. "Don't rush," he'd say as I reached for an invisible enemy.

Full-speed combat practice happened either at night or in the blazing heat of mid-day. The same instructions were given. "Relax. Don't rush."

"How am I supposed to not rush when I'm trying to hit you!"

"Relax."

"Argh!" I used my frustration to throw two quick jabs, both missed him, leaving just a sly smile on his face. I dropped to the ground and tried to take out his feet but he jumped, landing with his elbow in the back of my neck. I fell to the sand and felt it burn my cheek.

"Here, take this," Merl threw a long stick to me. I rolled over and stood.

"I've never used one of these before," I said, picking it up. The stick was made of blonde wood, and almost my height. Merl twirled an identical weapon in his well trained hands. I felt my heart dropping, this was not going to end well for me.

"Get a feel for it," Merl said.

I twirled it once feeling the even weight throughout. Merl jabbed at the air with it showing me how far it could reach. "See what this can do for you?"

"Sure," I mimicked his movement extending the weapon.

"Now bring it around." Using one hand, Merl spun the stick behind his back and then grabbed it with the other and brought it to his side. "You can defend yourself at a good distance from multiple attackers."

I smiled and followed his lead, bringing it behind my back and striking at imaginary opponents surrounding me. "Wouldn't a gun be even more useful?"

"Until you ran out of bullets."

I laughed. "That's what an extra clip is for."

"You know so much, do you?" I took my eyes off the stick and looked up at his calm face.

"Not so much. Just asking a question."

"I don't use guns, if you want to learn that you'll need to search elsewhere."

I shrugged. "Ok, touchy subject?"

"Guns make it too easy. Taking a life should not be so simple." He leapt across the space separating us and stopped just short of stabbing me in the stomach.

"If that was a bullet I'd be digesting lead right now."

"We are not actually trying to kill each other, Sydney," he said.

"Just play, right?"

"Exactly."

I hit his stick away using mine. His eyebrows jumped and he smiled at me. "That's it. Now what?"

I took a deep breath filling myself with the quiet of action. "Relax, don't rush."

He laughed and I went for his feet again. This time I got him! Merl fell onto his back and I rushed to take advantage of my position but he brought his stick up and I rammed my own stomach into it. I fell back gasping for breath onto the sand. "Don't rush," he told me, sand caught in his long, luscious eyelashes.

"Fuck you," I wheezed. He was already on his feet again. Merl reached out a hand to me, offering his help. I shook my head and rolled onto my hands and knees. We faced each other again.

"It was your brother's time," he said.

I spit sand out into the nearby surf. "What?"

"You heard me. It was his time; there is nothing you could have done. Everything is meant to be. Time-"

"No!" The anger came like a knife right through me. I struck at him with my stick and it clashed into his which was suddenly, inexplicably, in front of him. I stepped back and kept the weapon in front of my chest.

"You can't fix it, tape it up, extend it," Merl said.

I crouched down and swung the narrow tool at his ankles, trying to break him to the ground. He jumped and lighted back on the beach, as I tipped over with my effort.

"Time does not allow itself to be challenged."

I scrambled back to my feet, panting, sweat dripping into my eyes. He took a step toward me and I backed away.

"It keeps going and you don't."

I felt a blow to my arm that I didn't even see coming. It knocked me into the surf, my head went under for a moment, and I choked on the salt water. Jumping back up I was dizzy and disoriented, my throat and nose burning.

"And that is life," Merl said.

Salt water prickled on my skin and defeat closed around my heart. He stood in front of me, the wind playing with his ponytail, his big eyes looking into mine with utter calm.

I dropped my stick into the surf and walked up toward the Javelina. He took my feet out from under me and my chin hit the sand. I bit my lip and tasted blood. Rolling onto my back, Merl put the stick at my throat. "Are you giving up?" he asked, as gently as someone offering a cup of tea.

"I just need a break," I said, the chill water of the Sea of Cortez brushing against my feet.

"Another thing time does not give you. Do you see how full of wanting you are? And how little action you've got going on?"

"I don't even know what you're talking about half the time."

"Not so." We stared at each other for a moment. I licked at my salty, sandy lips and felt the grit in my teeth. "Get up," he said.

"How am I supposed to do that with you standing over me like this!" I yelled, anger so rich it seemed to be bubbling up past the sand, the blood and the sea water that lined my insides. He just smiled, the fucker.

"Not like that. Calmly. You always have an option. You're not dead until you are, so keep going. Fight me." His big brown eyes sparkled in the bright daylight. I swiped at the stick but he just pulled it up and then right down onto my throat again only this time harder so I felt like I couldn't breathe. I rolled away, tucking my head into my arms, rolling and rolling like I was kid playing roly-poly. Then I popped onto my hands and knees. He came at me and I threw up my arm brushing his stick aside. With my other hand I grabbed onto it and pulled it out of his grip. Keeping hold of the stick I backed up onto my feet. He was standing with his arms spread wide and his feet parted. We circled each other, both smiling at the challenge.

And so it went on like this. For one month, and then the next. We ran in the mornings and practiced fighting in the afternoon, then practiced fighting really slowly at dusk. Late at night, sometimes he would sneak into my RV and I'd have to defend myself from a state of sleep. You'd think after the first couple of times it happened I'd have trouble sleeping but I would hit my pillow every night and be out. The creak of the door, his footsteps, nothing would reach through my slumber until he was upon me. Once with his hands around my throat, another time it was a knife, on his third visit it was Merl's dog, Michael, that awoke me.

Michael was standing on my bed baring his teeth and growling. In the gloom of my bedroom I could see Merl in the doorway. "Wouldn't Blue be responsible for this kind of thing?" I asked. "Can't he take a shift?" I rolled away from Michael and tried to cover my head with a pillow and that's when I noticed the handcuffs.

"Blue won't always be around. You must learn to defend yourself."

"From a Doberman pincher who can put handcuffs on me?" I sat up and held my bound wrist toward him. Michael snapped at the air millimeters from my fingers. I pulled them to my chest. "Whoa, watch it," I said.

"What are you going to do?" Merl asked. "You look like you're getting angry."

"Ha, yeah, right," I took a deep breath because he was right, I was getting really angry. "Fuck!" I yelled before slamming my hand against the end of the bed dislocating my thumb with a sickening pop. The handcuff slipped off and I smashed the thumb back into place.

"Where did you learn that?" Merl asked.

I glared up at him, cradling my throbbing hand. Using the pain as a centering point for my thoughts I let my body do what it'd been trained for. Slipping off the bed, taking a small knife concealed under my pillow with me, I stood. Michael leapt at me. I side stepped, then pivoting my body, used the dog's momentum to slam him into the wall. Somersaulting over the bed, I landed inches from Merl with the tip of my blade at his throat.

"Well done," Merl said and nodded, smiling. "We will start with Blue tomorrow." Then he slipped from beneath my knife and disappeared into the night without a sound. Michael brushed past me as he followed Merl out. Climbing back into bed I looked down at my swollen thumb and the wrist that the handcuffs still hung from. "One day you'll thank me," Merl called from outside. I flopped onto my pillow and returned to sleep.

First we learned voice commands. When Blue moved from my left to my right in time with my calls, Merl made us do it with a whistle and finally silently - with only the motion of my hands to lead us. Soon our morning jogs included Blue running figure eights around me ("Circle,") retrieving sticks ("Boomerang,") or taking that stick to the right ("Blue Out"), or the left ("Brown Out"). We used the color of Blue's eyes as directionals because for the life of me I could not keep track of my left and right sides.

"Blue Out." Stick in mouth, Blue dashed up a dune and when he reached the top barked at me until I called him back ("Come"), or gave one long whistle, or held my right hand to my heart. He'd come racing across the sand, his teeth gripping the stick and a look of pure determination on his fuzzy brow. I grabbed it from him and Blue leapt around me filled with excitement. "Good boy, yeah, that's my good boy." I launched the stick into the sea and Blue dashed after it. Merl's three looked at him, and with a nod of his head, they joined Blue in the surf.

"He's an amazing dog," Merl said as we watched Blue pumping through the water toward the stick, the three Dobermans close on his tail.

"Yeah, I got lucky."

"You both did."

4

The Scream

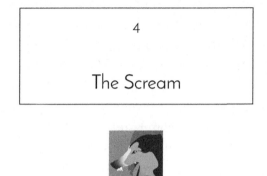

I WOKE UP BEFORE THE SUN. MY BODY FELT STIFF. Surprisingly, I wanted to go for a run. Consider my transformation complete, I thought as I stepped out into the hazy morning. Blue was overjoyed by my new need for speed. He circled me, letting out a bark of approval. It was as if he was saying, "See it's fun to run."

The sand was cool on my bare feet and the sun turned the sky and sea into the perfect heather grey as I trod along. My breath came easily, no panting and wheezing for me I thought with a smile. I felt strong. Really strong, like 'I could take on the world' strong.

As the sun rose bringing a pink flush to the sky my pace stayed steady. Blue and I ran where the sea and the sand met. Occasionally, I stepped into the gentle surf feeling a cooling tingle through my whole body as the chilly waters engulfed my feet. The beach curved around the shape of the land. How long had this been like this, I wondered. Did the shore line change every season as storms blew their powerful winds and slapped the beach with crashing waves or would the Mayans who originally inhabited this land recognize its topography?

Around the next bend we ran past a construction site still in the early morning light. It was one of those condo projects that promised the good life in the sun. And while I hated to see the land churned and the cement poured, I hoped that the people who moved here found peace and happiness. There was no place better than this for them to have a chance.

When my legs began to ache and my lungs swore they could take no more, I turned us back toward the oyster farm. Thoughts of a fresh breakfast with eggs and refried beans filled my mind as I pushed toward home. And home was what it was, I realized. In all my blind pain, pathetic misery and plain alcoholism, I'd managed to find the perfect place.

I slowed to a walk and felt the sun hot on my face. Blue jumped into the water and splashed out past where he could stand. With only a moment's hesitation I followed him. The water was cold and sent goosebumps spreading across my skin. It was the sweetest contrast to the heat burning through my muscles. I took a deep breath and dunked under the surface. Pressing my eyes closed, my hair floated off my head cooling me from tip to toe. I heard Blue barking through the crackle and shushing of the sea.

Coming up for air, I swam out to where my feet dangled without a bottom to touch. The ocean undulated around me guided by the moon and the wind. Blue's head cut through the crisp sea; swimming parallel to the shore, he steered toward the farm and I followed in a gentle breast stroke. Gulls cawed above us and the sweet mix of salt and sea wafted off the surface of the water. We moved slowly, the gentle swells lifting us up and down, quiet and calm under a clear blue sky.

The first scream was faint, followed by one fuller. Blue's ears perked in its direction and fear crept into my conscious. The thumping of my heart grew quicker and louder urging me toward shore. My toes sought the sandy bottom as Blue sped ahead. He emerged from the surf ahead of me. His thick coat hung on his thin form like an old forgotten fur coat. Blue shook, flinging off the weight of water in a 360 degree rainbow.

The waves pushed me toward the beach. Blue was waiting and once my feet hit the earth I took off at a sprint. Another scream, this one louder, was choked off by a sob. The sound forced me forward as I became convinced it came from the farm. It was a short distance before the small cement building and dilapidated plastic tables and chairs came into view. Two figures were standing in the bright sun, clutching each other.

Ramon and his mother. There was no mistaking his compact form, her long grey braid. She was crumpled against him, injured in some way I thought. Blue raced ahead when he spotted them. Neither looked up as he slid through the sand coming to halt by their side. The closer I got the worse it looked. Ramon's eyes were squeezed shut and an expression of utter pain distorted his features. His strong arms, muscles tight with tension, circled his mother, holding her up. The old woman's legs lay under her, limp and loose, her feet at odd angles in the sand.

"What's happened?" I asked, my breath coming in pulses. Neither of them answered. I touched Ramon's shoulder. His eyes shot open and stared at me but no spark of recognition lit them. "Ramon?" Tears welled and that sound I'd heard as a distorted cry in the ocean left his mouth in a wrenching scream.

Abedella leaned against Ramón's chest, listening to his cry through the muffle of his muscles and bones. "Let's get them inside," Merl said, suddenly by my side. He startled me. "A good lesson on how your emotions will blind you to your surroundings," he said. I stared at Merl, who stood there in the hot sun, calm and steady, not even a sheen of sweat on his skin. "Come," he said, turning to Ramon. Merl laid a gentle hand on his arm and Ramon turned toward the house, taking his mother with him. She stumbled along, never raising her face from her son's chest.

It was dark inside the cement structure. The small windows were shaded by the large palm frond roof that covered the dining area. The floor was immaculate except for the sand I dragged in with me. Normally I would have dipped my feet into the plastic tub of water Abedella kept by the front door but we'd rushed in here in such a fervor of excitement that I'd totally forgotten. I felt like an intruder watching their grief as they sat on their small couch, hands clasped, blank expressions on their faces. They'd told us their story, or at least what we could understand of it.

My complete lack of language skills was infuriating me. The dogs waited outside, all four of them panting in the shade watching the small house for movement. Once and a while I'd hear the soft padding as one circled the structure, the distinct sound of sniffing rising through the open windows. The horror of Ramon's story hung in the air. I could feel it like a weight against my body, squeezing me. Merl sat calmly on a plastic chair he'd brought in from outside.

Abedella hugged a photograph of the young woman, Ramon's sister, her daughter. It was in a cheap plastic, black frame that cut into Abedella's arms where she pressed into it. Paty was only 13 in the picture. It was a portrait from her communion. Paty was sweet looking. Overweight with tiny eyes, a nose so upturned it resembled a pig's and a weak chin made her far from beautiful but her smile was filled with hope and pride.

While everyone else in the room seemed to be stuck in some kind of time warp there was a rage building inside me. Who did this? Who trampled on these people's peace? These people who helped me without ever being asked. I stood up abruptly and went outside. Looking around at the empty tables and quiet setting I felt myself seething. This was not going to stand. Oh hells no. This was not-

"Sydney?" Merl was standing next to me. "Calm down."

I breathed deeply but all it did was fuel the power building in my chest. There was that core again, that excitement that was not going to let me or anyone else stop it. There was a yearning that could not be ignored. And whoever did this! They would pay!

"You can't help them in this state." Merl said.

"Don't worry. I'm going to help them."

"It's already happened. She is gone."

"I know that Merl!"

"Quiet," he hissed at me. "Do you want to upset them more?"

"I know she is dead. But I strongly disagree that there is nothing I can do. Why am I killing myself to learn all this if I'm not going to use it to help people like them?" I pointed back through the open door.

"You need to calm-"

"Go get your truck. We're going to Juarez." Merl opened his mouth to speak but I stepped right into his face. Eye to eye, I said in an even and deadly calm voice, "If you don't get your truck I'll go and buy one and I will take them there without you."

Merl cocked his head, examining me for a moment. "Okay," he said.

I went back to the door and communicated the best I could that we would take them to Juarez to help arrange for Paty's remains to be brought back and put to rest on the farm. I did not mention my murderous intentions.

I headed to the Javelina and changed out of my wet clothing and into a pair of cut-off shorts and a T-shirt. I threw on a hoodie and grabbed enough clean underwear and T-shirts for a couple of days. I also threw in a pair of jeans that Merl had made me buy because, as he put it, "they fit".

Within the hour we were on our way to Juarez. Merl drove, I stewed in the passenger seat, Ramon and Abedella sat like two over-used rag dolls in the back seat. All four dogs enjoyed the fresh air in the bed of the truck. "Usually Juarez would be considered a dangerous place to bring a truck this nice," Merl said. "But I think with all the dog power in the back we're going to be OK." He smiled at me and I tried to smile back but my mouth was set in a grimace and wouldn't even twitch.

"Malina," Abedella said.

I turned around. "What? Que?"

"Malina, Paty's amigo. She no good." Abedella nodded at her own judgement. Ramon shook his head but did not speak. "Malina make Paty go, she never want to leave me."

"No," Ramon said. "No."

Abedella nodded her head in agreement with herself and patted Ramon's hand. "No hablaremos de ella cuando la veamos. Esto es su culpa."

"What is she saying?" I asked turning to Merl.

He shrugged. "I think she is saying that they should ignore someone named Malina. That Paty's death was her fault."

"Does that make sense?"

"From what I understood earlier she was raped and murdered. Doesn't make a whole lot of sense that a woman did it."

"They move together," Abedella said leaning forward. "Paty never leave me. Malina make her go."

"Ok," I said.

It took us 12 hours to make the drive to Juarez. Merl suggested we stop and spend the night instead of fighting through but everyone else in the car felt it better to continue. The drive was bleak to say the best about it. Desert and scrubby shrubs lined the road. The occasional gas station and restaurant reminded us that we were still in a civilization. We stopped every couple of hours to stretch our legs and let the dogs take a break. I stared out into the desert with its pathetic dried-up looking plants clinging to life and tried to control the anger building with each breath.

It was dark when we got to Juarez. We found a hotel that accepted dogs and moved us all in. It wasn't a nice hotel but it was not disgusting.

Alone in my room I pulled the covers back and climbed under them, covering my head. Blue jumped up on the bed next to me and I heard his gentle breathing through the blanket. I fell into a restless sleep.

The following morning a knocking at my door woke me.

Abedella and Ramon stood outside dressed and ready to go. "Delegacion," Abedella said. When I stared at her blankly she said, "Police," and gestured that we should leave.

I nodded and held up two fingers to show it would just be a few minutes. "I'll meet you downstairs." They nodded their understanding. I grabbed my jeans and put on a clean T-shirt, brushed my teeth and hair, then Blue and I took the steps down to the lobby. Merl was there with his dogs. I almost laughed at the ridiculousness of him there. How many times do you get to see a guy with waist length curls wearing all black and holding onto the leash of three Doberman pinchers standing in the shabby lobby of a hotel? The guy behind the counter didn't find it as funny as me. He actually looked scared.

"I'll take Blue, why don't you escort them to the police station."

"Thanks," I said handing Blue's leash over. "Kinda ruins your look though." Merl just smiled.

The police station was only a couple of blocks away. It was early, and though the sun was hot, the sidewalk under our feet was still cool so the day seemed bearable.

The police station took up most of a block. Police cars lined the sidewalk. Some were pulled up onto the curb while others angled out into the street. The arrangement made it clear who controlled the block. A young woman wearing a dress that was almost appropriate for church but hugged a little too tight around her hips and pushed a bit too hard at her bust line stood next to the entrance. Ramon opened his mouth to say something to her but Abedella took his arm and hurried him up the few steps to the station's front door.

This must be the hated Malina - the girl who dragged their sweet Paty through the mud then got her killed, I guessed. I bet she'd always dressed like that. Some girls were born that way- it wasn't her fault. Paty's death was the sole responsibility of the men that killed her.

Malina clutched a small pocketbook to her chest as she watched Ramon and Abedella climb the steps and enter the police station. I went to follow them but stopped on the second step and turned back to the young woman. She was uncommonly pretty. Long, thick, dark hair lay shiny and straight down to her shoulder blades. And even though Malina's eyes were swollen and bloodshot from crying, their almond shape and rich hazel color still shone through. Full lips and a small nose completed her perfect little face. I wondered how much the disparity in their looks effected Malina and Paty's friendship.

I was staring at her for long enough that she shifted her attention from the closed doors of the station to me. "Hi," I said reaching out a hand. She looked at it and then back at my face. "I'm a friend of the family."

"I've never seen you before," she said, her English accented but very good.

"I'm a new friend." I dropped my hand seeing that she was not interested in shaking it. "I never knew Paty. I would have liked to have met her. I'm very sorry for your loss."

Malina nodded and mumbled a thank you.

I came back down the steps. "I'm sure you're anxious to see the murderers brought to justice." Her eyes widened and skittered around looking for danger. I followed her view and saw the dirty street, the old municipal building and the row of police cars. Malina's arm shot out and she grabbed at my elbow.

"Please," she said. "You are an American?"

"Yes, my name is Sydney Rye."

She shook her head, urgency playing across her face. "We are in danger here." Her eyes shot to the police station again. The building looked lifeless, like something forgotten. "Please, can you help us?"

"I don't know what you mean," I whispered back. If she hadn't looked so scared this would have felt like a game.

"Here," she opened up her purse and pulled out a card. Scribbling on it quickly she handed it to me. "Can you meet me here tonight? 8 o'clock?"

The card promised Margaritas by the yard and as many tacos as you could eat on Tuesdays. The logo was a sombrero-wearing mouse who appeared to be intoxicated. She'd written her phone number on the back. "Why?" I asked.

Malina lowered her voice even more. "I do want to see justice. Please."

"Okay."

"Thank you," she said. "I will see you there." Then she turned and hurried away from me. Several men pulling up in a police car swiveled their heads to watch her walk. I turned back to the building and, pushing the card into my pocket, ascended the steps.

Inside was stuffier and hotter than the street. Sweat dripped off the man sitting behind a desk in the full waiting room. Ramon and his mother were nowhere in sight. I must have missed them going in. The guy behind the desk didn't raise his eyes from his paper-work so I just took a seat next to an elderly man wearing worn jeans and a grim expression. A fan in the corner of a dusty windowsill ticked back and forth doing little to ease the heat.

It wasn't long before Ramon and Abedella came out. They looked stunned. Neither of them spoke as we walked back to the hotel. I didn't ask any questions. Merl was waiting in the lobby. Abedella and Ramon went to their rooms without a word.

"How did it go?" Merl asked as we stood waiting for the elevator.

I shook my head. "I don't know, they didn't say anything."

"Did you view the body?"

"They may have, I missed going in with them." Merl raised his eyebrows in question. "I met Malina at the station."

The elevator arrived. "Malina, the woman Abedella feels is responsible for Paty's death?" Merl asked as we got on. I nodded. "I'd say Abedella is as responsible for Paty's death as Malina."

"What?"

"Look," Merl turned his big eyes on me. "If Malina dragged Paty here I bet there was something pretty big pushing her. Neither of those two women are actually responsible for her death, that's not what I'm saying. Just that it's ridiculous for Abedella to accuse Malina. Everyone is responsible for this."

"Or just, like, one guy?" I said with a shrug. "The guy who actually killed her. Not those around her who loved her."

Merl sighed. "Obviously, you're missing my point. Sadly, it was probably some cops/drug dealers who did it for a lark after a drug run."

"I'm going to find them-"

Merl clutched my arm and yanked me to him. "And then what?" he whispered. "What will you do with them? Kill them? Murder?" I looked up into his eyes. "Well?" he shook my arm.

I leaned into him, pushing him backward. Merl almost stumbled but moved with me. I brought my hand up and rested it against his shoulder as we bumped gently into a wall. "Merl, don't talk to me like I'm an insolent child. Don't talk to me like I have not seen and done horrible things. This will not stand. Are we clear?"

Merl blinked his long lashes and nodded. I tried to back away but he'd slipped his arm around my waist and pulled me back close to him. He leaned his lips against my ear. "I prefer insolent children to murderers." I whipped my head around and our lips were almost touching when he said, "You cannot create justice out of hurt."

The elevator doors opened and Merl let go of me. I walked out into the hall. It was shabby with worn, brown carpeting and cheap wall sconces that flickered as trucks rolled by on the road outside. I showered, pulled on my jeans and a blue and white striped shirt. Slipping into my white canvas shoes I looked in the mirror. Another tourist, only with a few more scars.

I took a cab to the address on the card Malina gave me. The place looked deserted but had the smell of an often-visited bar. It was early still for a spot like this. The aroma of puke and stale beer was strong now but once you filled this place up with sweaty bodies it wouldn't smell like something old and used up anymore. If anyone was sober enough to smell the place it would probably reek of pheromones. Lots of young kids dancing, drinking, and looking for someone to fuck. I'd never gone for clubs like this; my wild nights were in smaller spaces, with intimate dance floors that it only took five people to populate. I was one for the basement bar on a freezing winter night. Or a candlelit garden on a warm one. This kind of mass entertainment was too obvious for me. The kids who would come here tonight to flirt and fight followed the same drumming of their hearts as I did but I liked mine a little more elusive.

And that's probably why I sipped at the beer I ordered. This place made me want to stay sober and get out, not drink up and get down. Malina puffed on her cigarette to get it lit. Smoke filled the air around her face. "I wish I could have done something," she said, laying the lighter down on the table next to her almost-empty glass. "If I had stayed I'd have ended up like her. On the side of the road, tortured, gone."

"Another?" I offered. She nodded. I caught a waitress as she hurried by and ordered another round even though my beer was barely touched. Nobody likes to tell a story drinking alone. "What happened to Paty?"

Malina looked up at me. Her almond eyes were bloodshot and the corner of one twitched. "You know it happens all the time here."

"I've heard."

"You've heard." She smiled but it wasn't a nice smile. It was a *'you've got a lot of nerve'* kind of smile. I sipped my beer. I could feel my face getting hot. The bar was humid and the crowd growing larger. "You know I moved out of there because I almost ended up like Paty." She pointed her cigarette at me and it vibrated with the tremble of her fingers.

"What happened?" I took another sip of my beer, feeling the coldness run down my throat and into my gut.

The waitress came back with our drinks and Malina pulled on

her cigarette, then looked up at the young woman in a tight white shirt and even tighter short shorts. "Gracias," she said, flashing a broad, happy smile. She could have been an actress, I thought. A great one. The waitress smiled back and then headed over to a table of recently arrived college kids. Malina watched her move across the room. One of the young men made a rude gesture at the waitress and Malina's grip tightened on the cigarette. "She is risking her life living in this city. We all are." She turned back to me. "Even you," she said, her mouth set in a tight line.

"You were going to tell me about why you moved."

She sat back and took a slug of her fresh drink. It was a pale yellow and on the rocks. "Paty believed that if she worked hard enough and played by the rules then she would come out on top. She thought that a company like Boeing would recognize her talent and eventually whisk her away to America."

She smiled and a tear escaped. Swiping at it, Malina continued, "You know many of us dream of that rich man who will marry us and take us some place wonderful. Paty felt that way about Boeing. She thought it was her ticket out of here. It turned out to be her grave." Malina pushed her half-finished cigarette into the ashtray and immediately reached for another. Her long fingernails were painted bright red and in the half light of the bar they looked coated in fresh blood. "I couldn't just keep working in that factory, waiting to die," Malina said, louder than she meant to. The boys over at another table fell silent and looked at us for a moment. Malina laughed and flashed them that smile. They grinned back and elbowed each other in excitement.

"You see," she said leaning across the table, lowering her voice. "I know the power I possess. I am not a, how do you say, small violet."

"Shrinking violet," I said.

"Yes, I am not a shrinking violet. I did not belong in that factory. Walking home in the dark. Living in a shanty town. Paty was foolish for staying. I tried to make her come with me."

45

"What do you do now?" I asked, having already guessed.

"I get paid, nobody rapes me, do you understand? I am the one in charge." Her eyes glowed with the passion she felt in this fact. "No man takes from me."

"So you moved out and started working in a different field," I said delicately.

Malina nodded. "I offered to pay for her to live with me." Malina's eyes filled with tears again. "She was my best friend." Her chin shook. She sucked on her cigarette and tried to shake the grief off.

"I'm very sorry."

"She was just so damn stubborn." Malina's fist came down hard on the table making our drinks jump. "You know her father was a monster. She couldn't do what I do."

"A monster?" I couldn't picture Abedella's husband being anything but sweet like her.

"That is why Ramón is like he is."

"What do you mean?"

There was a glaze to her eyes now, the second drink was almost empty and she finished it off before speaking. "Her mother was a sad drunk, same as mine. She'd just cry at the end of the night. I have heard my own mother cry herself to sleep, hiccupping," she said with disdain, "more times than I saw Paty's father turn violent. But I knew he hit sometimes. I'd seen the bruises on Mrs. Alvarez and guessed what they were from. Sometimes Paty would miss school and when she did come you could see the fading color where his fingers had gripped her arm." Malina reached up and rubbed at her bicep.

"But he hit Ramon the most. Ever since he was a little boy, I understand. And when Ramon was big enough he fought back and he won." Malina smiled at me. The waitress came over and Malina ordered another drink. I finished off the rest of my beer and nodded for another. The waitress left and Malina leaned across the sticky table toward me. "Ramon, he beat his father and kicked him, crying, into the dunes." She sat back and pulled on her cigarette.

"Mr. Alvarez, he came back the next day with a bat and beat Ramon so badly that he was never the same. A month in the hospital, his head all wrapped in gauze. It was terrible. Ramon was Paty's hero, her older brother, and after that, she was his caretaker."

"That's horrible," I said.

"At least Abedella got some sense into her after that. She would not let Mr. Alvarez home. He got very sick. The guilt, you know, I think it did something to him. He died in the street. I saw his body, you know? It took two days for the city to take it away. Paty saw it, too, and her mother. They refused to take it away. Said he was not theirs anymore."

"How old was Paty when that happened?"

"12, both of us, 12." Malina smoked her cigarette in silence until the waitress returned with our drinks. She took away our empties and Malina started talking again. "She was planning our escape from then on, you know? It's all she talked about from the time her father died until she did. The only reason I can speak English is because of Paty," Malina laughed. "She always made me practice, in our house we only spoke English. On the assembly line, everywhere. She said that if we wanted to move up in the world, we'd need English to do it."

"Smart," I said, sipping at my fresh beer.

Malina shrugged. "Not smart enough."

A large crowd of college kids entered the bar laughing and yelling. They filled the room and we heard them calling for shots and yards of beer.

"Paty was promoted you know, just three, maybe four, weeks ago. We went out for dinner to celebrate."

"How often did you see each other?

"All the time. She wanted me to come back to the factory and I wanted her to come and live with me and we were both mad about it but we tried to just not talk about those disagreements. We practiced our English. You know it felt like our special, secret language in a way. I know that is silly, but to us, it was special."

The waitress arrived with a tall glass filled with a thick drink topped by a slice of pineapple and a bright red maraschino cherry. "Del senor en la barre," she said to Malina placing it in front of her. Malina turned to the bar where a young man in a collared shirt and cargo shorts raised a shot to her and then downed it.

"One of my regulars. You will excuse me for a moment."

"Sure."

I sipped my beer and watched her approach the kid. He was drunk and so was she, both of them unsteady on their feet as they made it to the dance floor and ground up against each other. I shuddered at the thought of making my living by prostituting myself. Malina must hate it; for all her bravado, she must be slowly losing her soul. Then again, she may have lost it long ago. Maybe listening to her mother cry herself to sleep or running into the sand dunes to escape Paty's raging father sucked it out years ago.

Either way this night was starting to drag on. There seemed to be a lot of sad problems here but I didn't see any solutions or even the suggestion of one. When Malina came back to the table, her cheeks red and her neck slobbered on, I had lost most of my patience. Her beau returned to his friends at the bar and Malina, eyes glittering, waved at him. "Now that that's out of the way," I said, "I'd like to know why you invited me here. Do you know who killed your friend?"

"Why do you want to know? There is nothing that can be done." She reached for her pack of cigarettes again.

I stood up abruptly. "I'm sorry, Malina. I thought you invited me here because you were seeking justice, but it appears you're only interested in pity." I took out my wallet and began pulling out money.

"Please," Malina said quietly. "Sit down." I stared at her. "You're right," she continued, "I do want help. Justice."

I sat down. "Do you have a plan? Or even a suspect?"

"There were three of them. She never had a chance. She wasn't strong physically anyway. One of them could have overpowered her, let alone three. She must have forgotten her mace," Malina said, almost to herself, "Because none of them had red eyes."

"Malina?" She looked up at me. "Are you saying you saw them?"

"Yes." She nodded and reached for her drink, removing the pineapple and maraschino cherry, she took a long sip of the frozen cocktail. "Right after they came to the club, the one I usually work. They were bragging about it." She took another sip of the drink.

"Bragging about it?" I felt a chill run down my spine and land in my gut like a stone.

"Yes," she pulled out a cigarette and tried to light it but her hands were too unsteady. I took the lighter from her and lit the flame. She looked up at me and I saw through the haze of alcohol a deep and throbbing hurt inside of her. She leaned back with her cigarette burning. "One of them showed off the scratches on the side of his face while another made fun of him, asking what his wife would say. You see, to men, we are nothing."

"Not all men," I said.

"Every man I've ever met," Malina answered.

"What about Ramon?" I asked.

"Ramon is not a man. He is a child, a stupid child."

"No, Malina, he is a man who lost his sister and is grieving deeply."

"If he was a man, like the kind you imagine- one that cares about women - he wouldn't have let her come to this awful place. And if he could not stop her then he would be sitting with me now, seeking justice. Why are you here instead of him if he is such a man?"

"I'm more qualified," I said with more conviction than I felt.

"Will you help me then?"

"Help you do what exactly?"

"You're an American. Can't you do something? You just said you were qualified."

"What do you want me to do?"

Malina held eye contact with me and it was as if the room quieted around us. "I want you to kill them." The request hung in the air between us. She didn't say it like she was shy or afraid of the idea. She said it like it was a burning desire. When I didn't answer, she continued, "You don't understand what it's like to hear men joke about a girl they killed. Laugh at her fierce, yet feeble, attempt at living. You know they set her on fire while she was still alive? She screamed so loud that birds sleeping in a nearby tree took flight into the dark night rather than hear it through." Her hand shot out and grabbed mine. "Can you help me?"

Malina's regular separated himself from his friends at the bar and began moving through the thick crowd toward us. "Your friend is coming back," I said and stood. "Let me sleep on it. I'll call tomorrow."

Malina looked up at me and smiled. "I know you will help me. You are a good woman."

I laughed. "You don't know me that well." Leaving cash on the table I walked away right as the young man reached us.

Outside the night was cool and I shivered as a breeze blew through my lightweight shirt. Walking back toward the hotel I thought about what to do. Should I talk to Merl? Or would he just try to stop me? The likelihood of him offering help was zilch and he might even call Mulberry and tattle on me.

Back at the hotel I packed my bag quickly and, with Blue at my side, headed out into the night. A text to Merl let him know I'd see him back at the farm and not to worry. Then I powered off the phone paranoid he would track me.

I found another hotel, this one didn't even ask for my name. When I woke in the morning, my skin itched where bed bugs enjoyed my flesh. I used the phone on the bedside table to call Malina.

She sounded groggy and far away. "Malina, it's Sydney."

"Yes?"

"Yes."

She sighed, a soft sound through the crackle on the line. "When?"

"Let's get some breakfast. I need more details."

I showered, ignoring the scent of mildew and the mysterious stains that marred the once white tiles. Taking my bag with me I dropped my key at the front desk with no plans to return.

Blue and I passed by our old hotel. No sign of Merl's truck gave me hope that he had left, taking Ramon and Abedella home.

Malina waited at an outdoor cafe on the main strip. She looked beautiful, her skin fresh and eyes brilliant despite the early hour and the scent of last night's alcohol that clung to her. I introduced her to Blue then he settled himself under the table. "We can't really talk here," she told me, "let's get something to eat and then go to your hotel."

"I don't really have one right now."

"That is no problem. There are many."

"Sure," I looked at the menu for a moment. "Would it be okay if we put the room in your name?" She cocked her head in question. I shrugged. "There just might be some people looking for me."

"Okay. No problem."

Despite the restaurant's touristy location, the food was good and the coffee great. We didn't talk much over the meal, each lost in our own thoughts, but it was a companionable silence and at the end of breakfast, a closeness seemed to have grown between us.

We checked into a chain hotel that looked like a thousand others. Its blandness seemed to make us stick out more. As we waited for the elevator, I examined our reflection in the mirrored doors. Blue sat by my side, his tongue lolling out of his head. My new jeans fit me but not as well as Malina's. The denim that wrapped her legs appeared like a second skin. My loose linen shirt was wrinkled and almost the same grey as my eyes. Malina's halter top was synthetic and bright red. It matched the lipstick she'd applied as we left the restaurant. The scars that marred my face stood out pink and raw against my suntanned cheeks. Malina's skin was smooth and flawless. We were an odd threesome and I could see other patrons running their eyes over us looking for the connection. I doubted any of the business men in their lightweight suits and briefcases full of paperwork would figure it out.

In the room I filled a bowl of water for Blue and sat on the bed. "Tell me who we are going after here."

Malina sat on the bed opposite me. "There are three of them. Like I told you last night. All police, but they run drugs for the cartels. I know the youngest the best. His name is Adolfo."

"How old is he?"

"Just turned 21, graduated from the academy a couple of months ago. Benito, his uncle is one of the other men. Adolfo is under his wing."

"Who is the third man?"

"Frito. I used to think him handsome, but now…" she wrinkled her nose in disgust.

"Do you have pictures of them?"

"No, but I know where they will be tonight. They go to the cockfights."

"Cockfighting?"

"Yes, you have never been?"

"No." The idea sickened me a little. The irony did not escape me that I was getting queasy at the idea of two birds fighting while planning a triple homicide.

"They are very vicious, cocks."

I smiled despite myself. "Yes. I've heard that."

"Will you come tonight, and see them, the men?"

"Yes, I think that makes sense."

"They will be with their friends tonight so I do not think we can hurt them but maybe…"

"Let's just see how it goes. Opportunity may present itself. But it will probably make more sense to take them on one at a time. Why fight more enemies than necessary?"

Malina smiled. "Of course, that makes sense. We can get them in their beds."

"You know where they live?"

"No, but I can find out. Benito is married I know, with two children. Frito and Adolfo are younger and unattached."

I didn't want to hear about Benito's family. It was better for him to remain a shadow in the dark, an evil figure to be shot down rather than a man who might be missed. Malina seemed to sense my hesitation. "You do not need to worry about Benito's family. They will be happier without him. If someone had killed Paty's father, it would have been good for the world. Leaving those boys without Benito will make them better men."

"I hope."

Malina stood. "I will leave you now. Can you be ready at 8?"

"Sure." Malina started toward the door. "Wait," she turned. "What should I wear?"

Malina smiled. "You can go like that."

"I have a feeling as long as I'm standing next to you everything will be okay."

She smiled. "I feel the same about you."

Malina knocked on my door a little before 8. She was dressed in a tight pale blue dress that stretched over her curves and left little to the imagination. No one was going to be looking at me as long as I stood next to her. I was wearing my jeans, wrinkled shirt, and a baseball cap I'd picked up that afternoon. Blue tried to follow us out but I pushed him back into the room, figuring dogs were not welcome at cockfights.

We hailed a cab out front and when Malina gave the driver our destination he softly whistled between his teeth with disapproval. The cross swinging from his rearview mirror helped me guess where his judgment sprung from. We rode in silence, watching out the windows. It was a Saturday night and people were out and about. The streets glowed with white head lamps and red brake lights, illuminating the crowds of revelers as they moved from restaurants to bars. Men slung their arms over women's shoulders who smiled under the weight.

The taxi took us away from the traffic and crowds into the night. The sky was a dense cloud cover that reminded me of the matte-black color one of my mother's boyfriends had painted his pick-up truck. But while the original factory-applied blue still peeked through his paint job, God had blacked out the heavens without a patch of light in sight. The pavement under the wheels crunched with sand from the desert that surrounded the city. Out of the darkness rose a fairground, almost a mirage in that thick blackness.

"It comes at this time every year," Malina said. The Ferris wheel's bright lights seemed suffocated by the dense night. Strung bulbs looped between shacks that offered games of chance. I paid the cabby and climbed out. A man stumbled past me, tripping on his own feet and spilled some beer out of the plastic cup he gripped. "Pardon," he said, and then carried on toward a large tent at the rear of the fair. It's red and green stripes gave it away as our destination.

Children ran past in small groups, chasing each other, their laughter leaving a trail behind them. Malina glided through the crowd gathering the appreciative glances of every man we passed. The women on their arms scowled at her. I remained invisible. At the entrance to the tent, Malina flashed a smile to the man working the door and he pulled back the flap grinning widely.

The tent was packed with men drinking, smoking, and yelling. They all faced the center of the space where bright lights illumi-nated a ring painted half red and half green. In the center of the ring a man stood with a rooster held above his head. The crowd pressed toward him. I reached out for Malina's hand afraid that I would lose her in the squeeze. She laced her fingers with mine and pulled me through the crowd swiveling her head as she went. Men felt her touch and turned back with scowls until they saw whose touch it was. Once they'd had a second to take her in, they stepped aside allowing us to pass by without a word, some even took their hats off and nodded at her.

Closer to the ring were benches where fat men sat passing bills between each other. Cigars hung from their lips and pesos popped from between their fingers. The smell of money was thick in the air. We stood at the edge of the benches watching. A fat fuck with greasy skin and thinning jet black hair stood in the center of the ring holding a rooster. He took the bird over to another man who appeared to be a judge of some kind. Short and sober-looking, he was tying something to the rooster's legs. Malina leaned into me. "He is attaching the spurs."

"Spurs?"

"They are sharp knives. And now you see-" The little man picked up a lime and squeezed it onto the spur. "He does this to get rid of any poisons that the owner might have applied. They fight to the death so it is very important that the fight is fair."

A second man stepped into the ring, a white rooster struggling in his grip. The first cock, armed and ready was handed back to its owner. The second man was handsome in a slimy kind of way. His broad shoulders drove sharp lines into the world around him. There was nothing wasted in his face, a roman nose and deep brown eyes placed above just the right amount of cheekbone. His shirt was buttoned-down and freshly pressed, his pants fitted, but not obscene. "That is Frito," Malina told me. "He comes to where I work often. His looks are considered very fine."

"How are his cocks?" I asked.

Malina laughed.

After taking his bird to the referee who attached the spurs and sprayed the lime juice, Frito, cock in hand, faced the other owner. They pushed the birds at each other, who squawked and clawed at the air. The crowd leaned forward and there was a final rush to place bets. "Benito is there," Malina said, tilting her head to our left. "Next to him is Adolfo, the young man. And his children too." I scanned the crowded benches until I saw a big man with a paunch sitting next to a stone-faced youth his junior not only in years but in girth. Two boys on the cusp of puberty sat next to Benito, their faces lit up with excitement. Benito rested his arm on the closer boy's shoulder and smiled down at him. In his other hand he held a half empty beer. Adolfo, the young man, leaned against his elder and said something into his ear. Benito nodded and pushed his chin toward the exit. Adolfo got up and worked his way through the crowd. I lost him as he disappeared into the sea of men and boys pressing toward the spectacle.

A cry went out and I looked up to see the sand floor kick up dust as the two cocks charged. They met in the middle, airborne, like Greek gladiators. Their legs kicked as their wings flapped behind them. The spurs sliced through flesh and feathers, gushing bright red blood on the ring's dirt floor. The white bird lay still as the referee pulled the other cock off. It was over.

Money flapped between sweaty palms as bets were paid and collected. "It was so quick," I said.

Malina nodded. "It often is."

Frito stood looking down at his dead bird. The winner held his bird aloft, the man grinned broadly, his cheeks ruby. I turned back to Benito who sipped from his beer and smiled at the scene. His youngest boy leaned across and asked him something. Benito nodded his head and the youth hurried off into the crowd.

Adolfo returned, his face a mask. "That guy does not have much expression does he?" I asked Malina. She turned her attention from the ring and looked over at Adolfo.

"No, he is one without many words."

"What's his deal?"

"His deal?"

"His story. Like, who are his parents, where does he come from?"

"He is an orphan, since he was very young, I think. Follows Benito like a dog."

"Does he partake at your club?"

"Only on occasion. The boy does not seem to be one for pleasure."

Adolfo was saying something to Benito which was clearly making the older man upset. He shook his head, then shrugged his shoulder and nodded. Benito looked over at Frito and I followed his gaze. The handsome man was picking up the bird's corpse; he tossed it over the side of the ring.

"I was once here with a customer," Malina said. "He was from China and told me that in his country, it is considered a great honor to eat the dead bird. But here, we just throw them away."

Benito caught Frito's eye and he started toward him. Benito stood and said something to his son then handed him some bills. The boy smiled and pushed the money into his pocket. Frito joined Benito and Adolfo, all three men headed toward the exit.

Malina followed them, taking my hand. The air cooled as the press of the crowd eased. Outside we spotted the three men under a tree that looked like it was the only one for miles. All three men held cigarettes. Malina and I stood in the shadow of the tent and watched the burning embers move up and down with each drag.

"If I sneak around I think I can hear them," Malina said, and then before I could respond she disappeared into the night. I stood still under the starless sky ensconced in shadow and watched the three murderers of Paty Vaquez. It took most of my will, and all of my might, to control the emotions roiling inside of me.

Benito, the sturdiest of the figures under the tree, dropped his cigarette to the ground and twisted it under his boot. The other two followed suit and started to move toward the parking lot. Silently Malina appeared by my side again. We watched as the killers climbed into an SUV. The headlights lit with the rumble of the engine and they pulled out past the games and rides toward the open desert.

"They have another girl," Malina said. "They are holding her in some abandoned buildings outside of town. I know where it is."

I nodded.

"We must help her," Malina said, her voice high and anxious.

I looked around the parking lot. "We need a ride. A pickup would be best."

"I do not know any taxis that are trucks." She pulled out her phone. "I can call around."

I shook my head. "That one will do," I pointed to a black truck in a spot near the rear of the lot. Mud splatters proved its rugged nature and the rust that pattered its side panels made me think it wasn't anybody's baby.

"Ah, I see." Malina looked around the lot suspiciously.

"Don't do that," I said. "Act natural. Come on." I walked toward the truck like I owned it. Not that there were many witnesses to my stroll. The tent was packed and anyone outside was much more interested in the rides and games than our trip across the parking lot.

Approaching the driver's side, I pulled on the door handle but the owner was smart enough to lock his doors. Malina went around to the passenger side and found another locked door. "What do we do?" she asked.

Old trucks like this you could usually pop with a simple wire hanger but I didn't have one. "Does your bra have an underwire?" I asked Malina.

She sighed and I figured this was not the first time her undergarments had been used in the process of a crime. She was on the hidden side of the vehicle and with a couple of well-practiced moves, was out of her bra. I heard ripping and then she passed the thin wire over to me. One quick glance around to double-check no one had noticed our behavior and I slipped the wire between the window and the doorframe.

It took me about ten seconds to pop the lock. The click of success was a wonderful sound. Reminded me of an ill-spent youth.

This was the first time I'd ever needed to steal a car. My skills were honed joyriding. What boredom will do to the teenage mind....

I climbed in and unlocked Malina's door. She hopped in and smiled at me. "Now comes the hard part," I said inspecting the ignition. "Any chance you have a screw driver in your drawers?"

Malina laughed. "No, but I have a nail file."

I looked up to see her holding it. "Brilliant." I used the nail file to get the truck going. Only one of the headlights worked and the thing smelled like sweat, meat sandwiches, and spilled beer but it was our ride and I was proud of myself for stealing her. I pulled out of the fair and headed back toward town.

"Turn left," Malina said.

"I've got to pick up Blue first."

"Okay," Malina agreed. I pulled the aging pickup truck in front of the hotel and left it running while I ran in to grab Blue. He was excited to see me and happily jumped into the back of the pickup when I patted on the truck's bed.

"Head back toward the fair," Malina told me. I watched Blue enjoy the fresh air in my rearview mirror as we drove through the congested streets. However, once we were out of the city and picked up speed Blue laid down, becoming invisible to the world. "What will we do if we find them?" Malina asked.

"The important thing is to help the girl."

"Yes, but how? There are three of them and two of us."

"I've got a gun, a dog, and the element of surprise."

"I've got a gun, too."

I glanced over at her. "That's good," I said.

She nodded at me. "Thank you for your help."

"Thank me if we survive, okay?"

Malina nodded.

Past the fair, the night engulfed the road. Malina pointed ahead. "Turn there." I slowed down and pulled on to a rutted road which lead into the rocky hills that line the US/Mexican border. There was no sign of life as we bounced down the path.

Blue stayed low in the back and Malina clutched the door handle to steady herself. Up ahead the road cut between boulders. My visibility was shortened by the sharp turns so when I came around a bend and saw the SUV blocking the road I had to slam on my breaks. Our truck kicked up dust and pebbles as it slid to a stop.

I barely had time to register the figure running toward my open window when Blue launched himself onto it. They went down, Blue on top, the man under him screaming. Slamming the old truck into park, I opened my door and began to pull my gun when I saw Benito taking aim at Blue. It only took two steps to grab his arm and aim the gun toward the sky. He looked at me with rage-filled eyes.

A shot rang out into the night, the sound bouncing off the boulders around us. "Put it down!" Malina yelled. I struggled to maintain my hold on Benito's gun. We were both clenching it. "Sydney, let it go or he'll kill me," Malina spoke again.

I turned to see her standing in front of the one working head-light of our truck. Adolfo was behind her, his thin frame shielded by her curves. He pressed a silver pistol to her temple. I saw his lips move in her hair. "Call off the dog and let Benito go," Malina said through trembling lips.

Blue was holding Frito on the ground. Frito was yelling and with each new outburst of sound, Blue shook Frito's gun arm again. The pistol lay in the dirt a few feet away from where they struggled. "Blue, Out!" I yelled, as I felt Benito gaining control over the gun. Blue's eyes landed on my face and he hesitated for a moment. "Out!" Blue released Frito's arm and, grabbing the fallen gun in his mouth, shot off between two boulders.

I stepped away from Benito letting him have the gun. He smiled and threw a punch at my face. Instinct made me knock it away and elbow him in the back of the head as the force of his would-be-blow sent him by me. Benito fell to his knees and Malina screamed.

I looked over to see Adolfo wrenching her head back. She gurgled as he forced the gun between her lips. Benito scrambled to his feet. "On your knees," he said. Blue began to bark. Benito swiveled his head looking for him. "Shut that dog up," he said, starting toward me. I held my hands up. He grabbed me by my collar. "Shut that dog up!"

"I can't," I said.

"I'll kill you," he said, pressing his pistol under my chin.

"Look," I started, "you can kill us now or you can take us some place nice and enjoy your time. Either way, that dog is not going to stop barking. So why don't we all just take a drive in your SUV? Somewhere you can't hear the dog and we can work this out."

Benito laughed. "Work this out." He let go of my shirt. Frito was struggling to rise and Benito went and grabbed his good arm hauling him up. "You are going to pay for this. You came here to kill us, no? You wanted justice." He laughed again. "How could you think that we would not hear about you and your pathetic little plan?" He walked back over to me. Blue's barks continued their steady rhythm. "What a fool." I closed my eyes and let the blow come. It knocked me sideways. Benito followed that with a blow to the back of my head that dropped me to my knees. I hovered on the edge of consciousness for a moment before he hit me again and everything went black.

THE PAIN PRECEDED CONSCIOUSNESS. Blinking my eyelids sent ripples of hurt across my face, around the back of my head, and down my neck into my shoulders. I heard myself groan.

Forcing my eyes open I tried to focus them. My chin was resting on my chest and I was looking down at my wrinkled linen shirt. Slowly I was able to make out the fabric's grain. The splotches of blood dripping from my nose made me feel the itch of dried blood on my cheeks.

With a Herculean effort I lifted my head and tried to take in my surroundings. It appeared I was alone in a large, empty room with a high ceiling. There was a doorway in front of me pockmarked with holes and standing slightly ajar. Moonlight streamed through the opening's landing onto a dusty, uneven wooden floor. There were two windows on either side of the door coated in dirt so thick I couldn't see through them. I sat on a wooden chair with my wrists bound behind me.

I looked over my shoulder and saw I was wearing handcuffs. Looking down I saw that my ankles were chained to the chair legs. I took a deep breath and silently thanked Merl for all the times I'd woken up pinned to my bed. I gritted my teeth prepping for the excruciating and awkward pain. I struggled not to cry out as I slammed my thumb against the chair.

My hands free, I leaned over to inspect the chains that bound my ankles. These guys were either amateurs or had severely under-estimated me. I stood up, my head spinning, and sat back down.

Reaching up, I found the source of all that blood on my shirt and the dizzy spell. A clotted mass of hair and an open wound was at the base of my skull. When I touched it I almost threw up. I took a minute and a few breaths before trying to stand again.

The chains tinkled as I attempted to rise. They were wrapped around my ankles and in-between the legs of the chair. All I had to do was pick up the chair and shake off the chains to be free. Granted, my ankles were still chained to each other but at least I wasn't stuck with the chair.

With my new freedom, I walked over to the windows on the far wall. Peering through a broken pane, I saw another building and an alley lined with tall grass and trash. Hearing a scrape behind me, I wheeled around.

Merl was standing there, leaning casually against the decrepit wall. Blue charged toward me and after sitting at my feet, leaned against me. I crouched down and embraced him. Merl's three dogs flanked him, their eyes reflecting green in the darkness. "One thing we didn't go over was how to not fall into a trap," Merl said. "Obviously, you still have some things to learn."

I smiled at him. "I am really happy to see you."

Merl pushed off the wall and crossed the room. He approached the window and peered through its grimy pane. "Did you really think I was going to let you get yourself killed?" he asked without looking at me.

"I'm fine. But thank you for coming."

"You're not fine. You're holed up in an abandoned building hunting mass murderers. Alone." He craned his neck to get a better look the base of my skull. "With a head wound."

"Well, I didn't think you'd want to help."

He turned toward me. "I don't."

"Then what are you doing here?"

He smiled. "You didn't leave me any choice."

I bit my lip. "Well, thank you. I appreciate it."

Thunder, who'd stayed by the entrance, gave a low growl of warning. Merl crossed the room without a sound and looked out into the night. "The young one is getting something out of the SUV." I heard the thunk of a car door slamming. "He's headed back inside."

"What did he get out of the truck," I asked.

"A chainsaw."

"Jesus," I said.

Merl leaned against the wall and rested his hand on Thunder's head. Clouds shifted and the pale light of the moon was blocked. A cool breeze blew through the open door stirring up the smell of sawdust.

"Did you have a plan?" Merl asked.

I smiled. "Plans are God's favorite joke."

Merl smiled. "Okay, well, what's the joke of the evening, then?"

"Not sure. I just woke up and managed to free myself."

Merl looked down at my ankles. "You're not that free."

"I don't have a chainsaw," I smiled.

Merl chuckled.

"What's the deal, where are they?" I asked.

"There are three of them. They are holding Malina there." He pointed across an expanse of cracked pavement and weeds at a large building. It appeared deserted with broken windows and patches missing from its roof. But a light burned inside, bright in the dark desert.

"They took my gun," I said "I don't see how we can get close enough to these guys for hand-to-hand combat."

Merl smiled, showing off his big-gapped teeth. "I brought my throwing stars." He opened up his trench coat to reveal a vest lined with multi-sided blades. "Quiet, accurate, deadly. More than I can say for your pistol."

I realized my mouth was hanging open and snapped it shut. "That is seriously awesome."

Merl nodded. "I know."

"Will you teach me-"

He held up a hand to stop me. "Let's see how we do here. If we survive, I'll think about it."

"Right. If we survive."

"I did bring you a weapon, though." Merl reached under his coat and pulled out a long knife. A strong wind blew across the desert and whipped around the building pulling dust with it. The door banged on its hinges and Blue growled at the sudden movement. The bluster passed as quickly as it arrived and an eerie silence fell over the compound. "Now or never," Merl said, handing me the blade. It felt heavy in my hand and I looked down at my bound ankles. "Just remember to take tiny steps," Merl advised, following my gaze. I nodded.

Merl tapped his hip and headed out of the door. His three dogs lined up behind him. I followed them, shuffling, trying to contain the clinking I made. Blue stayed close behind me. Merl moved across the broken pavement of the parking lot barely making a sound. The whirl of a chainsaw broke the silence, followed by a woman's scream.

Merl sped up and hunkered under one of the building's dirty windows. He motioned me down and I crouched by his side. Sliding up the side of the building, Merl looked through the window.

"I see two of them," he said just loud enough for me to hear over Malina's terrified screams. Merl lowered himself back down. "Take a look."

I rose up until I could see into the room. It was large and lit by fluorescent fixtures that stretched the length of the space. The one closest to the door flickered, casting a light of unreality onto the whole scene. Malina was tied to a chair, she had swelling around her mouth and her dress was ripped open exposing one of her breasts. Malina's rich hazel eyes were glued to the whirling blade of the chainsaw which Adolfo held in front of her. His back was to the door but I suspected he wore the same stony expression as at the cockfight.

Benito was pacing behind Malina. He was saying something I couldn't hear. Not far out of Benito's reach was a small table covered in tools and I spied my pistol. Scanning the rest of the room, I didn't see Frito.

"Here is what we are going to do," Merl said. I tore myself away from the horrific scene inside and concentrated on Merl's plan. "What we've got is the element of surprise, you, me and four dogs."

MERL KICKED IN THE DOOR, Benito looked up from his ranting, opened his mouth, and then brought his hands up to his neck. Blood spilled from between his fingers and dripped off his lip. Adolfo spun around to face us as Thunder and Michael led Lucy and Blue down the sides of the room. I was right about Adolfo's face. He just saw his uncle die and there was not even the hint of emotion across his brow.

Merl launched another throwing star but Adolfo blocked its path with the chainsaw. It went wild and flew across the room breaking out one of the few remaining window panes. Blue and Lucy turned to the center of the room headed for Malina while Michael and Thunder waited for Merl's sign.

Blue knocked into Malina sending her backwards, hard, onto the floor. She grunted but did not complain. Lucy grabbed the tatters of her dress and started pulling. Blue took hold of her jean's cuff and helped move her away from danger. Adolfo looked over at me and narrowed his eyes. He turned to check on Malina and saw her being dragged away. Adolfo almost went after her but saw Merl playing with another throwing star and thought better of it.

Merl let out two sharp whistles that launched Thunder and Michael into action. They lowered their heads and approached Adolfo from behind, snarling and snapping their teeth. Adolfo turned around and waved the saw at them but the dogs continued their slow approach.

Merl nodded his chin at Adolfo's exposed back. The clanging of my bonds would have given me away except the chainsaw was sucking in all the sounds. Adolf was swinging the monster back and forth at Thunder and Michael. Blue and Lucy barked from the corner they'd dragged Malina to.

My baby steps carried me within striking distance. I lined myself up with his small frame and with one more step, wrapped my left arm around his shoulder. He tensed momentarily and tried to turn toward me but I had attached myself to him. I brought the knife against his throat, quickly drawing it from one side to the other.

Adolfo dropped the chainsaw and brought his hands up to his neck. I felt a gush of wet warmth on my arm. The chainsaw spun out of control on the dusty floor, its engine whining. Adolfo fell to his knees. My arm was still gripped across his shoulders and I stumbled forward with him. I used my fist, still gripping the knife, to push against his back and right myself. Adolfo fell to the floor, his eyes fluttered and then lay open as blood spilled out of his neck.

I approached the chainsaw when another explosion of sound distracted me. It was Frito and a gun. He'd burst out of somewhere holding something metal in front of his torso and was racing across the room firing a gun at me. I saw him stumble and change his aim to Merl who was crossing the room with long, powerful strides, his trench coat billowing out behind him. His arms moved like a machine firing off stars as fast as Frito's bullets left their chamber. But unlike Frito's bullets, Merl's weapons found their mark. Frito fell to his knees and continued to squeeze the trigger of his empty gun. "Mercy!" Frito yelled as Merl, without missing a step, pulled out a full-size sword from within the folds of his trench coat. With one clean stroke, he sent Frito's head across the room.

"Jesus," I said, but no one heard it over the sound of the wild chainsaw. Bending down I grabbed its handle and turned the thing off. Through the silence that descended upon the room I could almost hear the blood pooling. Merl looked over at me and tilted his chin toward Malina.

I hurried over to where she lay on her back, knees and feet in the air. "Malina," I said as I approached her. She couldn't see anything the way the dogs had her surrounded.

"Sydney! You survived. Oh, thank God." I crouched by her side and saw tears running down her cheeks. "You got them. You really did, didn't you?" She was smiling and crying.

I nodded. "Yeah, Malina. They're dead."

She started to sob, her shoulders shaking. Merl whistled and Lucy left us and ran to him. I sat Malina up and inspected her bonds as she continued to sob. Lucy returned with a key ring in her mouth. I looked over at Merl but his head was down as he searched the large room. I found a handcuff key and freed Malina's wrists. When I came around and knelt to work on her ankle chains Malina threw her arms around me. "Gracias! Gracias!" She cried onto my shoulder.

I stiffened at the sudden embrace but soon responded, wrapping my arms around her shaking form. "Okay," I said, "it's okay."

She pulled away and wiped at the tears on her face. "I must be a mess."

I laughed. "You're not even dressed," I said.

Malina looked down at her ripped dress and laughed, too. "Here, I'll give you mine." I started unbuttoning.

"No, no, I'm fine."

"I'm wearing a bra," I pointed out. "You donated yours to the cause of almost getting ourselves killed." Malina smiled. "Please," I said, taking off my shirt and putting it over her shoulders. She nodded and her lip quivered with emotion. "Shhh. It's okay." She nodded again and I started working on the locks that attached her ankles. The key ring was massive but I started with the small keys and found it soon enough. Once she was free, Malina helped me with my chains.

The smell of gasoline reached my nose and I looked up to see Merl spilling it out of a large container onto Frito's headless corpse. "Come on," I said, standing up and offering my hand to Malina. She took it and I pulled her up. I walked over to where Merl was leading a trail of fuel to Benito's body. "Do you need help?" I asked. He looked up from his work.

"No, why don't you two wait outside." He looked down at my bra and his eyebrows scrunched, then looking over at Malina, he figured it out. "Here," he said, putting down the gasoline can. "Take my jacket."

"I-"

He held up a hand. "I'm not arguing with you about this, Sydney. Jesus. Just accept some help when you need it." He jerked his jacket at me.

"Sorry."

"Fine." He picked up the gasoline can and continued his work as I wrapped the trench around me. It smelled like sandalwood and musk. I turned toward Malina who was standing over Adolfo looking down at him. "Come on," I said, taking her by the elbow.

She looked up at me. "I wish they would feel the burning." I squeezed her elbow and with one last glance at Adolfo's corpse, she followed me outside. We waited by the SUV in the parking lot with Blue, Lucy, Michael and Thunder who kept a vigilant watch. The moon was waning and I suspected it was no longer late but rather getting early. Merl came out with the tank, leading a trail to the SUV. He splashed some onto the hood and then stood back.

Pulling out a road flare from his back pocket he was about to crack it when Malina said, "Wait." Merl paused. "May I?" She reached toward the flare. Merl looked at it, then over at me. "I just want to do something. I wish I could have killed them, you know?" Malina said.

Merl handed her the road flare and stepped back. Malina snapped the stick to life and looked down at it for a second before tossing it onto the SUV's hood which ignited instantly. We backed up toward the open desert and watched the flame whip toward the building. It went through the open door and started as a glow, but soon the flames were licking at the roof and the building raged. Windows exploded, walls crumbled, and the sun began to rise behind it, paling in comparison.

SAYING goodbye to Malina wasn't easy but Merl insisted we leave immediately. He didn't want me going back to a hotel covered in blood. "And besides," he said. "With your concussion, you can't sleep. I'll keep you awake while we drive. Do you like show tunes?"

Malina looked over at him. "Is he serious?"

"I don't know," I answered. "I'll walk you to your door."

We stood in front of her apartment and she tried to give me back my shirt but I shook my head. "I know it's not your style but what am I going to do with a bloody shirt?"

Malina smiled and stopped fiddling with the buttons. "If you ever need anything, you call me, okay?" she said, tears welling in her eyes.

"Listen," I licked my lips trying to figure out how to say what I wanted to say. "I'm going to take care of you."

"What?" Malina cocked her head.

"I'm going to set you up with an account and you won't need to worry about money anymore. You won't need to hope for a man to take you away. I'll give you enough to take yourself away."

"How?"

"Just trust me."

"With my life."

"Yeah, me too. Thank you, Malina."

"No-"

I put my hand up. "Thank you for being brave enough to ask me for help."

Her lips quivered then leaning forward, Malina hugged me. "Thank you."

"Good night, Malina."

"I will see you again."

"I hope."

WE STOPPED AT A TRUCK STOP. Merl went in and got a clean T-shirt for me and some first aid supplies. Then Merl did some doctoring work on the back of my head. He also brought me Ibuprofen which was keeping the pain down to a dull ache.

We couldn't make the whole drive back in one shot. Merl got too tired and I was struggling to keep my eyes open. Merl pulled off the highway and put his seat back. We both passed out immediately. When we woke it was dark again. By the time we made it back to the Oyster Farm, it was light. There was a rental car parked next to the Javelina. Merl stopped the truck and turned to me.

"I'm going now."

"What?"

"This is over," he said, wobbling a finger between the two of us.

"But I'm not ready."

Merl laughed. "Tell that to the three corpses in the desert."

"But I never would have survived without you. And how will I learn to throw throwing stars!"

Merl smiled but didn't budge. "Sorry, Sydney. Mulberry is pissed at me. And you. But he loves you, so will forgive you soon enough. Me on the other hand, I've had enough shots fired at me for one day."

"No, Merl, I don't want you to go." I reached out and took his hand. He looked down at it.

"I'll miss you, Sydney."

"You don't have to, you can stay."

"Neither of us can stay, Sydney. We have to move on. Please be safe. And ask for help when you need it and..."

"I will Merl."

I reached across and hugged him. "Thank you," I said into his shoulder. "Thank you for everything."

I pulled away and opened the truck door. I looked back at him and leaned across, quickly pressing my lips to his cheek. I felt the stubble of his two-day-old beard and smelled musk then hopped down from the truck.

Blue jumped out of the back and I waved as Merl turned the pickup around and headed back through the dunes.

INSIDE I FOUND Mulberry asleep on my bed. I paused in the doorway to watch him for a moment. The man's gentle breathing brought me peace. I noticed new sprays of gray at his temples and felt a pull at my heart.

I sat on the bed next to him and reached out to touch his hair but pulled back and rested my hand on his shoulder instead. His eyes blinked open and he smiled when he saw me. "You're killing me," he said. "You're really driving me up the wall."

I shrugged, unconcerned with his mental health.

"You're going out murdering police?"

I laughed. "They were killing, raping, drug-running machines and I stopped them. Killing police. Listen to yourself, Mulberry. So moralistic."

His face reddened. "You can't just go around killing people," he said sitting up.

"They were hardly people."

"I'm sending you to London for more training and I need to know that you're not going to go apeshit on me every time someone gets hurt."

"What are you talking about Mulberry?" I was angry now and stood up. "I'll do what I want to do. This is not some game where you get to call the shots. This is my life."

Mulberry climbed off the bed and faced me. "A life I gave you."

I felt the anger seething in my chest. "You gave me? Where would you be without me, Mulberry? Where? At home, on your couch in New York watching sports, wishing you had the balls to be anyone else?" I took a step toward him but he stood his ground.

His face was turning deep red. We were both very angry. I wondered for a flash if it would turn into a physical fight, only inches separated us.

"I think you know that you couldn't have done it without me," he said

"Yeah, and you couldn't have done it without me, so don't go around thinking you're special and I'd be destitute without you."

"How about we're even," he said gruffly, casting his eyes to the floor for a brief moment and then back up to my face. "How about we stop fighting?"

There was something so sweet in the way that he said it, I almost laughed. But instead I nodded stiffly and took a step back.

"They were bad guys, huh?" Mulberry asked.

"Yeah," I nodded. "Really fucking bad."

"Alright," Mulberry said. "You get packed and I'll drive us to the airport. We've got a flight in a couple of hours."

"Really? That quick? I don't know if I can be ready." I looked around the cramped RV and saw that really I didn't have much to take. No reason to bring my pathetic assortment of pot and pans. My clothing, what there was of it (shorts, ratty T-shirts, a worn pair of jeans, a couple of sweatshirts) would all fit into a small duffel.

"You don't need much. We're going to have to get you some new clothing once we get to London so just grab a toothbrush and whatever personal effects you have and let's go."

There was a small case in the bedroom which held a couple of pieces of jewelry I inherited from my grandmother, a photo album that showed my family in much happier times. Everything fit into a small knapsack and I left the RV with it.

The day was bright and I walked slowly toward Ramon's house. I stopped and stood in the hot sun for a long moment. Sweat pooled in my lower back and I squinted in the heat. I never said I would stay, why announce that I'm leaving? Don't be a schmuck, I thought, and continued to the small home.

"Hola," I called, but no one responded. I knocked and pushed open the front door but no one was home. It was cooler in the cement structure. I put down my bag and pulled out a piece of paper and a wad of cash.

My pen hovered over the blank page. What could I say to this man and his generous mother? They took me in with no judgment. No questions. They let me be. How few people we find in this world who will offer you that space. "Thank you," I wrote, "You will always be with me." Then I put the money in the center of the note and folded it up. I left it sitting on Ramon's worn plastic chair.

Back out in the heat of the day, Mulberry was waiting in the car with the air-conditioning on. Blue was in the back seat, his head resting on the armrest next to Mulberry. I settled into the buttery leather and we took off into the dunes.

"You probably won't do anything like that in London, right?" Mulberry asked as we pulled onto the paved road.

"Yeah, probably not. I don't see the government turning against its own people there."

He looked like he wanted to say something, but bit his tongue at the last second. I could almost guess what it was. That even if the government did turn against its own people, there wasn't much I could do about it. Killing people only makes you feel better, it rarely solves the problem.

Kurt Jessup dying didn't bring back James, and those crispy corpses in the desert didn't bring back Ramon's sister. Time will not be swayed or discouraged. It marches on and on with no thought of righting wrongs or delivering justice. Killing might be my best, but it wasn't good enough.

<<<<<<<>>>>>>>

Turn the page to start reading an excerpt from
Insatiable (A Sydney Rye Mystery, #3), now.

SUNSHINE ON A SUNNY DAY

Carlos was the one who felt my phone vibrating; it was under one of the napkins we'd used for our picnic lunch. I found it, and glancing quickly at the "UNKNOWN" on the caller ID, picked it up. While used to calls from unknown places, I was not used to calls from this guy.

"Sydney, how are you?"

I didn't actually recognize his voice right away. I rolled away from Carlos, sitting up. "I'm sorry, but I don't know who this is." It was when he laughed that I recognized him. "Bobby?"

He laughed again. "I'm glad you remember me. My heart would be broken if I could be so easily forgotten."

I stood up, Carlos looked up at me, a question in his eyes. I shook my head and stepped away from our blanket. My dog, Blue, a huge wolf-like creature with one blue eye and one brown followed me, keeping at a heel. "Forget you, Bobby Maxim? In order to do that I'd need a lobotomy."

"With your penchant for revenge, I half expect to see you bursting through my closet doors some day, guns blazing."

I laughed. "Who says I'm not in there right now?"

"I know exactly where you are. I've been keeping very good track of you."

I looked around the park. Gentle green hills spotted with couples and groups of friends lounging on blankets dominated the landscape. On a field below me a soccer match was beginning to form. A woman ran by in a skin-tight suit, nothing on her jiggled.

"Are you here now?"

"No, no. I'm calling to ask a favor."

"That's rich."

Someone tapped me on the shoulder. I spun around and stepped back. Blue let out a growl. Carlos stood behind me, his hands out, palms forward in a sign of peace. "I just wanted to let you know I'm going to join some mates for a game of football."

"Sorry, that's great. I'll see you in a bit," I said, covering the mouth piece. Carlos smiled and jogged off down the hill.

"Does he know about you?" Bobby asked. I didn't answer as I watched Carlos join a group of other men on the field below. "Sydney, are you there?"

"I'm not doing you any favors. I don't know if you're totally clear on the fact that you took something from me."

"Sydney, I don't understand this animosity. I was just doing you a favor."

"A favor!" I heard myself yelling. Looking around I saw that I'd attracted the attention of several of the groups of Londoners trying to enjoy their first day of sun. "You bastard," I hissed quietly. "I hope you rot in hell."

"I'm sorry I didn't do it sooner, darling."

"Call me darling again and I will make it my life's mission to take your ball sack. Are we clear?"

"Anything you'd do with my ball sack would be very welcome."

"I forgot what a sick fuck you are."

"A sick fuck who did you a favor and is now looking for one in return."

"You're insane!" I heard myself yelling again. I took a deep breath. In through my nose, out through my mouth. Blue tapped his muzzle against my hip to let me know he was still there.

"Sydney, I didn't know what you two had planned. I would have killed Kurt long before you showed up. Remember, I'm not the one who left my fingerprints behind; whose blood was spilled all over the floor. You took yourself down, it had nothing to do with me." He said it in an off-hand way. Like I was being petty and missing the big picture.

"You killed him," I whispered, trying to control my anger, but I could feel myself shaking. "That was my right. Kurt Jessup murdered my brother and I should have been the one to end him."

"At the time I had no idea about that. Mulberry didn't tell me what you were planning, just that we had a problem. I had no intention of stifling your little revenge act. If anyone should be pissed it's me. At least you got the treasure."

I stood on the green feeling lightheaded. It was like Bobby Maxim was taking the world and flipping it upside down. "What are you talking about? Mulberry told you that?"

"Oh Cher, you didn't know?" Maxim's voice rose an octave, teasing and dripping with syrup. A cold knowledge traveled from my toes right up to my brain, my best friend betrayed me, our relationship was built on a lie. I walked toward the shade of a tree, reaching out to rest a hand against the rough trunk. "Mulberry called me, told me about Kurt. About him killing Tate and Joseph," Bobby paused, "about how he killed your brother, James." I picked at the tree in front of me, breaking off a piece of the bark. I looked at the white underneath, the exposed inner branch. "Now don't get all upset and quiet on me, dear. He only did it to save you."

"Save me?"

"From becoming a killer."

"You think someone can be saved from that?" I heard sadness in my voice and hated myself for it.

"No, I don't. I think you are what you are, Sydney. And I think it's amazing. I want you on my team."

Click here to continue reading
Insatiable (Sydney Rye Mystery, #3).

About the Author

Emily Kimelman is the author of eight Sydney Rye Mysteries, she also co-authors the Romantic Thriller Scorch Series, and is working on a fantasy series due out in 2017. She lives on an airstream with her husband and daughter—they follow the sunshine, great hiking and good food... oh and wifi. Lol!

She shares their adventures on Instagram, Facebook and in her Readers' Group.

Sign up for Emily's Readers' Group to get free books, all her updates and never miss a new title!

If you've read Emily's work and want to get in touch please do! She LOVES hearing from readers.

www.emilykimelman.com
emily@emilykimelman.com

A Note From Emily

Thank you for reading my novella, *Death in the Dark*. I'm excited that you made it through my bio right here to my "note". I'm guessing that means that you enjoyed my story. If so, would you please write a review for *Death in the Dark*? You have no idea how much it warms my heart to get a new review. And this isn't just for me, mind you. Think of all the people out there who need reviews to make decisions. The children who need to be told this book is not for them. And the people about to go away on vacation who could have so much fun reading this on the plane. Consider it an act of kindness to me, to the children, to humanity.

Let people know what you thought about *Death in the Dark* on Goodreads and your favorite ebook retailer.

Thank you, Emily

Want More?

Visit www.emilykimelman.com for a complete list
of Emily Kimelman titles.

Made in the USA
Las Vegas, NV
14 April 2021

21406977R00052